A Night to Remember

AN ADAIRSVILLE HERITAGE MYSTERY

Danny and Wanda Pelfrey

CrossLink Publishing
RAPID CITY, SD

Pelfrey/CrossLink Publishing
1601 Mt Rushmore Rd. Ste 3288
Rapid City, SD 57701
www.CrossLinkPublishing.com

Ordering Information:
Quantity sales. Special discounts are available on quantity purchases by corporations, associations, and others. For details, contact the "Special Sales Department" at the address above.

A Night to Remember/Danny and Wanda Pelfrey. —1st ed.
ISBN 978-1-63357-422-9
Library of Congress Control Number: 2022930763

CHAPTER 1

"**D**o you think of Nate as a grandfather or, perhaps, uncle?" the interviewer asked.

"No, not really," Kaylene answered without hesitation. "I have three uncles and, thank God, I still have one of my grandfathers. Nate is just Nate. He doesn't replace anybody. He's just always been part of our lives."

Riley was glad that Kaylene, one of the girls from the Sunday school class she taught, had asked her to stand in for her working mother and accompany her to this interview at the Maggie Mae Tea room. She too was curious to learn the story behind Kaylene and her family's friendship with Old Nate Bannister.

Riley had learned shortly after arriving in town that Old Nate had retired from a long and successful baseball career more than thirty-five years earlier; he was as close as Adairsville had to a celebrity. From time to time, she had seen him and Kaylene walking down Main Street— "Nate and the Kid," as they were known by friends and family. The Kid was usually talking a mile a minute with a soft drink or candy bar in one hand, while the burly old man moved slowly, his posture straight as an arrow and his attention focused straight ahead, apparently ignoring the babbling kid at his side.

Riley and Kaylene were here today because the county commissioner's life had recently come to an untimely end. Nate, to almost everyone's surprise, decided to throw his hat into the ring. Despite his age and lack of previous experience in politics he had respect and name recognition, so he had to be considered a serious candidate. Susan, the young reporter from the *Daily Times* in Cartersville, had learned of the

"Nate and the Kid" angle and thought it might be an interesting twist for her upcoming article.

"Tell me about how your family first became friends with Nate," the reporter requested.

"Nate bought the farm while still playin' baseball. He hired my dad to run it. They worked together in the off-season, mostly raisin' cattle, chickens, hay, and sometimes corn. Mom and Daddy lived in the little house where Nate lives now. My two brothers were both born while they were there. Then Nate retired from baseball and later, when his wife passed, he got bored with farmin'. Mama has always said he practically gave Daddy the farm. My parents and brothers moved into the big house where Nate lived. He moved into the little house. That's the way it's been ever since. First my sister, Ella, came along and then me; that was after Mom and Daddy were in the bigger house. We've been neighbors, friends, and, I guess, family with Nate through all those years."

Riley turned when she heard the jingle of dishes being gathered for removal from a nearby table. A middle-aged lady in a blue apron smiled at her. "Anything I can do for you?" the waitress asked.

"We're fine," Susan called back before looking at Kaylene. "How did you personally get to be so close to Nate?"

Kaylene looked upward and held her mouth tight for a few moments. "My mama always said it started when I was a newborn. She said I was a colicky baby and Nate was the only one who could get me to calm down. I guess there has been a bond between us ever since. As far back as I can remember, I followed him around when he helped Daddy on the farm, doin' the things that must be done on a little farm like ours. From the beginnin' he called me "the Kid" and now just about everybody but my friends at school have picked that up."

"For as long as I can remember, I've wanted to be a nurse. When I was six years old, Nate opened my nursin' school account at the bank and has been addin' to it ever since."

"Did Nate and Mrs. Bannister have children?" Susan asked.

"Well, yes they did. They had a little girl, but she died when she was two years old. That's what Mama and Daddy told me, but I've never heard Nate talk about her. I don't know, but maybe I sort of took her place."

"Back when you were a little girl following Nate around on the farm, did you know he had been a big baseball star?"

Kaylene cleared her throat before answering. "I don't think I did at first. But then I noticed men always wanted to talk baseball with him. Maybe I picked up on how famous he was when I started listenin' and askin' him a lot of questions about it. Daddy says those sports writers are crazy for not puttin' him in the Hall of Fame." Kaylene raised her voice. "He won 247 games, you know, and that was while playin' with three teams at the bottom of the standings. He'll go in some day when that veterans' committee finally come to their senses," she declared with conviction.

"How do you feel about Nate possibly becoming county commissioner?"

"Daddy says he's out of his mind to take on all that aggravation, but Nate thinks somebody needs to step in to protect people's rights. If that's what Nate wants to do, then I'm all for it. He's a good Christian man who cares about people."

Riley was impressed with how her little friend was handling the interview. She felt almost ashamed that before today, she had silently questioned the uncommon relationship of the twelve-year-old girl and the old baseball player. After listening to Kaylene speak of it, she understood their alliance in a different light. Obviously, it was the kind of family bond that only occasionally develops between two people not connected by blood, but by circumstance. There was certainly nothing improper about what Nate and the Kid had. Previously, she had wondered why no one seemed to have reservations about such an unusual friendship. Now she knew. It was simple: the town knew Nate and the Kid well. She, being relatively new, did not—until today.

The interview lasted for another half hour. Before it ended, Kaylene had both Riley and Susan in stiches by telling hilarious stories of her family's life with Nate. Riley was sure the old man would just about die of embarrassment if any of Kaylene's tales ended up in print: like the account of his being chased by an angry bull or the story about his backing his car through a stuck garage door when he was late for an appointment. Her own impression of Nate as a humorless, dignified old man obviously had been totally inaccurate.

What a unique and delightful bond the two characters at different ends of life's cycle shared. Riley was grateful for the rare opportunity to see into the life of one of her favorite Bible school students.

She drove Kaylene to her family's farm after the interview. The twelve-year-old stayed in character all the way home and didn't stop babbling until they arrived at the farm. Sam Boynton, a lean, middle-aged man with dark skin that was obviously the result of long hours outside, greeted them in front of the big farmhouse. "How did it go, Kid?" he asked his daughter.

"It was fun, Daddy. She's a nice lady. She said we should be sure to get a paper on Friday." He turned to Riley. "Sorry we had to call on you to escort Kaylene, but Wilma couldn't get off from work, and I was needed around here. There wasn't much doubt about who she wanted us to ask. Yours was the only name she mentioned. She surely does admire you!"

"I was glad to do it. It gave me the opportunity to get to know Kaylene better. You would've been proud of the way she handled the interview. She's a special gal."

"I've known that for a long time," Boynton remarked as he used one arm to pull Kaylene close to him. "Now, young lady, you need to go into the house and change so you can help me with some chores in the barn. Thank you for your help today, Miss Riley. You've been a blessing to us."

Riley thoroughly enjoyed the rural scenery on the five-mile trip back to town. Having grown up in the greater Boston area, she had not experienced a great deal of what the rural South had to offer. She would always be grateful for what Uncle James had done for her. In his generosity, not only had he left enough money for her to complete her education, but he had also left her and her brother Kirby a church building converted to a living space that had become her home for the past year. Throughout the school year, she often drove the seventy miles from Emory Law School in Atlanta to spend her weekends there. Now she would have almost three months of rest and relaxation in the little town that her deceased mother and father had so loved. That would be made even better in a couple of weeks when her brother would join her permanently in the quaint little hamlet. She had not tried to influence his decision, but she could not be happier that he had finally chosen to give up his position with the St. Petersburg, Florida police department to oversee the family businesses.

On top of that, her favorite friend from her time at Boston College was traveling to Florida to visit a mutual friend and would be arriving that evening to spend a few days with Riley. Trish Banks had decided to drive from her native Massachusetts rather than fly. Riley wondered how Trish really felt about flying and laughed to herself as a couple of Trish's ridiculous phobias crossed her mind. How could she forget climbing up twenty-five flights of stairs in a New York building because Trish didn't trust the elevator, or the night they got no sleep during an exam week because she thought she saw a spider? It would, no doubt, be an interesting few days with her peculiar, but lovable, friend.

Before going back to her living quarters, Riley decided to go by the office to visit with Connie Reece. Connie had been selected to serve as the administrator of the extensive business interests that Riley and Kirby had inherited from their Uncle James almost a year earlier. Gradually, Connie had assumed most of the responsibilities from the semi-retired Amos Edwards for managing the Gordans' hardware stores, lumber yards, apartments, rental houses, investments, management properties, and other concerns. Keeping it all finely tuned was a big job, and the vivacious Connie did it well, especially for one so young. She was also Kirby's on-and-off-again girlfriend. Presently their romantic relationship appeared to be somewhere between on and off. That didn't affect the couple's working relationship, and it didn't alter her and Riley's friendship; in fact, she had grown to consider Connie her best friend. Now that Kirby would be a full-time resident of Adairsville, she hoped the two would work through their little love spats. A late fall wedding would be delightful, she decided.

When Connie was hired, she, Kirby, and Amos had decided to put her office on the second floor of a building Uncle James had purchased in the middle of Public Square. Prior to that most of the work had been done out of the revamped church building where Riley was currently living. Amos and Carol had living quarters along with separate units for Riley and Kirby. She loved living in the same building with Amos and Carol who had become sort of surrogate parents for both her and her brother.

As usual, Riley found Connie hard at work at her computer. "It's time to take a break, girl," Riley called out as she entered the office.

"If you say so," Connie responded. "You're the boss."

"I wish you would tell Kirby and Amos that. They think I should take my monthly check, study hard and leave business to you guys. Just a pretty face, you know."

"I've got a feelin' that when you finish law school, you'll get plenty of opportunities to do your share."

"That's still two years away. I'm going to have a lot of catching up to do. I assume we're still on for tomorrow night?" Riley said while looking out a window to watch several people visiting in front of the old railroad depot. "I can hardly wait for you to meet Trish. She's a riot! I just know the two of you are going to be fast friends. I think we'll go to the Adairsville Inn. Need to introduce Trish to some of our local color."

"Sounds great to me. Do you have dates lined up for all of us? I haven't been out with a date in several weeks."

"I'm sure that will be rectified when Kirby gets here," Riley smiled.

"I don't know," Connie said. "I haven't heard from him in several days. He's probably spendin' all his time on the beach with some Florida babe."

"You know better than that. He has eyes for only you. If I know my brother, he's probably spending eighteen hours a day trying to wind up every unsolved case he's had down there."

"Incidentally, would you tell Amos I received a report from a neighbor that someone has been seen the last couple of days out at that old, dilapidated house that sits on the edge of the woods? You know the one I'm talkin' about. It sits on the property y'all own on Snow Spring Road. I don't think there's much chance of anyone doing any damage unless they set it on fire and ignite a forest fire, but somebody could get hurt on the premises. And since it's so isolated, you never know what's going on out there. I think we ought to tear that place down."

"I'll deliver your message when I get home, and I'll tell Amos you suggested we get a demolition crew in there sometime soon."

The two ladies drew glances from several men on the street as they headed downstairs to the General Store and Mercantile Cafe for a tea break. Skylar, the friendly young waitress, there alone during the midafternoon lull, hurried to their table to take their order for two ginger peach teas, which were quickly delivered.

After leaving the café, Connie returned to the office while Riley headed for her car and drove home. When she saw Amos's pickup sitting in the driveway, she decided to deliver Connie's message before she forgot. "How was the interview?" Amos asked when after hearing her knock, he opened the door to see her standing there.

"It was an interesting experience. Kaylene is a sharp little girl, and she sure does love old Nate."

"Always has," Amos replied. "They've been inseparable about as long as she's been able to walk."

"I stopped by to visit with Connie. She told me to tell you a neighbor spotted someone hanging around that old house on our property just off Snow Spring Road. She suggested you might want to check it out. She also expressed her opinion that the house probably should be demolished."

"I'll investigate it. How do you feel about tearing down the old place?" Amos asked.

Pleased that Amos had asked her opinion concerning a business matter, after a moment, she answered, "It serves no purpose. Well past restoring, I suspect. If it doesn't have any historical significance, let's remove it before it becomes a problem."

"I think you're right. Tomorrow, I'll see if Bill can go out there with me. Maybe he and his boys can do the job." Bill, Juan, and Jessie were the workers who comprised the Cleaning Crew, a branch of their business that handled maintenance and such. All of them, along with their families, had been homeless before being discovered last summer by Riley and Kirby. Now they were not only employees, but good friends as well.

Riley crossed the hallway on the second floor of the former church to enter her own apartment. With Trish due to arrive tonight, she decided to inspect her little guestroom one last time. She wanted everything to be just right for her guest.

Trish had been more than just one of her college friends: they were roommates for their last two years in college. Riley had even spent the summer between her junior and senior years at Boston College with Trish's family in their big house near the Massachusetts coastline. She had often talked with Trish over the past year, but had not seen her since she and Kirby had first come to Adairsville to settle their uncle's estate. They had expected to be there less than a month, but had been captivated by the hills of northern Georgia and their delightful people. Adairsville had become home for her, and, even though she had a hard time reading her complicated brother, she thought it had for him as well.

It was almost six o'clock when Riley laid down her book, went to the kitchen to make a sandwich, and brought it back to her sitting room along with a few chips and a diet coke. She gave her attention to the news on TV while munching her not-so-healthy dinner. After a few minutes, she thought she heard a car entering the drive. Then she heard a horn, and she knew immediately it was the unconventional Trish announcing her arrival. She ran down the stairs and through the door to find Trish standing beside the open car door. Trish immediately started running toward her with arms outstretched. As they embraced for a big hug, Trish began squealing and talking a mile a minute, all at the same time. Riley could do nothing but weep with joy.

CHAPTER 2

A man with slicked back hair and pricey workout garb was riding one of the gym's stationary bikes when his phone rang. He checked the screen, then dismounted the bike and moved into a corner of the room where his call could not be overheard. "Yes," he answered, keeping his shrewd, clear voice low.

"This is Houston!" The voice on the other end of the line was just the opposite—raspy and boisterous. "Is this the boss?"

"Yes, you clown, this is the boss. What's going on? I told you, unless there was a real problem, you were to wait for my calls each evening."

"I reckoned you would want a report on where we are with our project. We've got the kid."

"What kid?" The boss inadvertently raised his voice. He checked the room to make sure no one had heard him.

"The little girl that hangs with the old man. We've got her tied up right here in this old house in the woods where we've been stayin'. My old lady is keepin' close tabs on her."

"You fool, I said nothing about kidnapping a kid. I told you I wanted you to make sure the old man would not be in the election."

"That's what we're doin'. I've already used the kid's phone to call her daddy. I told him if the old man didn't pull out of the election in the next week, he would never see his little girl again."

"Why didn't you just take the old man out? Snatching a kid can get you in more trouble than you can shake a stick at."

"They tell me the old man packs a .38 Special, and he knows how to use it. He's a pretty tough old turkey. No danger in grabbin' the girl out of the barn. The easiest way to go, we figured."

"I'd just as soon you let me do the figuring. I don't care how you do the job. I just don't want that ole man in that election. He's got a good chance of winning, and we can't let that happen. Just remember that I don't want anything you do to lead the cops back to me. If that girl fingers you, I had nothing to do with it. You hear me? You are on your own."

"She'll never finger anyone again. We've got to keep her kickin' until the guy pulls out. We might have to prove to her folks that we still have her. But after that . . ."

"I don't want to hear about it. Do what you must and when it's all over, you need to get as far away from here as you can, as quickly as possible. I'll call you tomorrow evening."

You get what you pay for, the boss thought. *Never again will I hire for a job based on the bottom line. I've made some dumb moves in my time but hiring that buffoon may be the dumbest of all. Well, maybe it'll work out, or I could end up in prison for the rest of my life . . . or worse.*

***

After she and Trish used most of the night to catch up, Riley rose at 8:30 to start the coffee before rousing Trish, which proved to be no small task. After eating a breakfast of bagels and cream cheese, they took turns showering and dressing. "How do you do it?" Trish asked when she came out of her bedroom. "You stay so fit and trim. I have to work out and diet all the time to maintain this," she said holding her arms out and looking down at her body. "Nothing I do makes a dent in the extra twenty pounds I carry around."

"I think you look great. You've got to remember I'm five inches taller than you."

"I know, not every gal can be a supermodel like Riley Gordan."

"Don't sell yourself short, Trish. You're one of the most beautiful people I've ever known."

"Here it comes—the speech about how beautiful I am on the inside. I want to be beautiful on the outside too. I want my phone to ring all the time, the way yours did when we were in college."

"The operative word is *did*," Riley responded with a smile.

"What's the matter, are the guys not harassing you like they did back in Boston?" Trish laughed. "Are you seeing anybody? What about that policeman you talk about? What's his name? Mike? Mike Unger, is it?"

"Mike and I still go out occasionally, but we're just friends," Riley insisted.

"Maybe in your mind you're just friends, but does Mike see it that way?"

"I think he would like for it to be more. He's a good man, but with law school and everything I've got going, I'm just not ready for that kind of relationship."

"Be careful you don't wake up someday realizing you're ready, but it's too late," Trish cautioned with a serious look on her face.

"I've got to take you down the hall to meet Amos and Carol," Riley said, anxious to change the subject. "You're going to love them. I don't know what I would have done over the past year were it not for them. I'm sure you'll have an opportunity to indulge in Carol's southern corn-bread and vegetable soup along with her sweet tea while you're here. That alone is worth the trip to Georgia."

"Just what I need," Trish declared, "more calories."

When they rang the Edwards' doorbell, Carol opened the door and hugged both of them. "Such a beautiful girl!" she declared, stepping back to take a good look at Trish.

She may be a grand lady, but so much for her honesty, Trish thought. "Why, thank you, Lady," she said with a curtsy.

"Is Amos not at home?" Riley asked.

"No, he left about fifteen minutes ago to run down Bill. He said something about getting him to go out to look at an old house."

The ladies spent the next hour talking and laughing. Carol showed off the more than one thousand thimbles she had acquired over the years, among other collectables. Trish was fascinated by the advertising inscribed on most of them—everything from cotton gins to tearooms. As they were leaving to take a tour of the town, Trish remarked gleefully to Riley, "You're right, she's wonderful. I can't wait to try her soup and cornbread."

***

Amos found Bill and his crew preparing an apartment for a new tenant. The tall crew chief was busy trying to lift a spot off the carpet in one of the bedrooms. "Do you have an hour to take a look at an old house we need to tear down?" Amos asked. "If you guys can do the job, it would mean a good hunk of extra cash on your paychecks."

"Juan and Jessie aren't going to like me skipping out on them for an hour, but they'll live with it if they know it could lead to more money."

The two men traveled west in the gray Dodge Ram pickup on narrow country roads for more than ten minutes before coming to an unpaved gravel drive. They were on the rough drive for less than a quarter mile when they came over a hill and suddenly saw a sad little house with peeling paint and the front porch leaning to one side. Amos knew no one had lived there for at least five years. That was when James had bought the fifty acres on which the house stood. Back then he had made the decision that the house wasn't worth saving, but there had been no hurry to raze it because, being isolated, it bothered no one. James had sometimes talked about getting into the cattle business and one day came up with the idea that the old house might be a good place to store hay, but Amos doubted Kirby and Riley would be interested in running cattle.

Amos parked the truck close to the dilapidated porch. He had never found a good reason to walk further than he had to. After getting out of the truck and closing the door, he thought he heard a noise coming from inside. "Did you hear that?" he asked Bill.

"I did," Bill answered. "Better be careful, there might be some kind of animal or maybe even a family of animals in there."

"Yeah, a year ago, I saw a bear not far from here." Amos stopped to pick up a broken bottle and throw it away from the house. Neither man seemed to be in as big a hurry to get inside as they had been a moment earlier.

When they got to the door, the two men looked at each other as if to ask, "Who's going to go first?" Suddenly they heard an engine start from behind the house. Amos ran through the house to the back door he knew to be in the old kitchen. Bill followed. As Amos passed through the open door, a metallic green Kia Soul was disappearing around the side of the house. Amos caught a glimpse of a girl with her face pressed against the glass of the back seat window on the passenger side. *That child looks familiar.* "Go out the front door and see if you can get the number on the license plate," he yelled to Bill.

Bill ran to the porch, but by the time he got there the car was going over the little hill. "I'm sorry," Bill told his friend. "Too far away to see the plate."

"That's okay, they'll probably stay away now that they know they've been spotted." *Who was that kid in the back seat?* "That's it!" Amos mumbled to himself. "It was the Kid. It was that Boynton girl."

"Did you say something?" Bill asked.

"Just talking to myself. I think I know that girl in the back seat. She and her folks go to our church. You've seen her. She's the little girl that hangs around with Nate Bannister, the ole baseball player."

"The little girl that never stops talking," Bill said.

"That's a pretty good description," Amos laughed. "I wonder what she was doing here. Her folks aren't the type to trespass and run, and I'm sure they don't have a Kia."

Looking around the front room, Bill noticed wrappers, bags, and cups scattered on the floor. "I would say some homeless people have been staying here, but for two things."

"What two things?" Amos asked.

"First, people who are homeless don't usually set up housekeeping this far away from civilization. Makes it hard to get food. And, secondly, they don't usually have a car. Sometimes, but rarely. When they do, they normally live out of it. To me, this looks like someone hiding."

The two men spent a few more minutes looking over the little house. Bill was sure he and his two cohorts could do the job. Their work calendar should clear enough for them to get started in about three weeks. "The only problem with us working this far out is going to be keeping Jessie in the required coffee and donuts."

"I've noticed Jessie has put on a few pounds since you guys have been with us."

"We all have. It comes from eating regularly."

***

Riley and Trish were in the garden when Amos parked his pickup. No doubt he was drawn there by the talking and laughter coming from that direction. He appeared with the big smile for which he was famous among the people of Adairsville and beyond. "This must be the lovely Trish," he surmised.

"In the flesh," she responded with a wink. "And who is this perfectly handsome southern gentleman coming our way? Could it be the celebrated Amos Edwards of whom I've heard so much?"

"I don't know if I can stomach all the bologna being tossed about in this garden today," Riley said. "Trish, we'll not be able to live with him for a week if you keep trifling with him like that. He already thinks he's God's gift to the women in this town. Don't encourage him."

"Don't you listen to her," Trish shot back. "I meant every word I said." She took two more steps toward the now beaming gentleman and embraced him. "I'm thrilled to meet you, Amos."

"It's my pleasure to meet you, young lady. Riley has told us so much about you. We already love you for being such a friend to our girl."

"Some people are just easy to be friends with. I always figured being pals with her was good for my image."

When Amos did not immediately come into the house, Carol came outside to see what was going on. The four continued their visit for a few more minutes. Before they went inside, Amos got a bit serious. "Riley, Bill and I went to the old house off Snow Spring Road a little while ago. As we were going into the house a car sped from out back. The garbage we found in the place led us to believe that the people in the car might have been spending a lot of time there. That doesn't surprise me, but there is something about the whole episode that did throw me for a bit of a loop. There was a child in the back seat of the car that looked like Kaylene Boynton. I could be wrong. I only had a quick glimpse, but it sure did look like her. The car was a metallic green Kia Soul. I would say an earlier model."

"That's strange," Riley responded with a puzzled look. "I was with her yesterday. Why would she be out there? And with who? Nobody in her family drives a Kia."

"I know. That's why it all seemed so out of focus to me. I didn't report the trespassing because I didn't want to get anybody in trouble."

"I'll look into it, Amos. I'll give her a call and see if I can find out what's going on."

Having slept little the previous night, Trish decided to take a nap before they left to meet Connie at the Adairsville Inn. Riley tried to call Kaylene but got no answer. She tried again fifteen minutes later; still no one answered. *That's odd. Kaylene is never without her phone for very long. Why is she not answering? Maybe she made the connection to Amos when he saw her, and she's afraid or embarrassed to take my call. That's probably it.* Riley had the phone numbers of all her Sunday school students, but not their parents. She would try Kaylene's number one more time before they had to leave for the restaurant.

After a while, Trish appeared in the sitting room and tried to make conversation, but Riley seemed somewhat detached. "You're worried about that girl, aren't you," Trish asked.

"Yes, I am. I've tried to call her a couple of times and gotten no response. I'm going to try again." This time Riley heard the voice of a woman on the other end of the line, one she did not recognize. When Riley asked to speak to Kaylene, the woman harshly told her there was no Kaylene there and she was to stop calling. Then she disconnected the call, not allowing Riley to probe any further. "This is really bizarre," Riley told Trish. "That is Kaylene's number. I called her at that number yesterday. I have no idea who that rude person I just talked with was." After mulling it over for a couple of minutes, she said, "Let's go get Connie and drive out to the Boynton farm before we go to dinner. I need to know what's going on."

Riley called Connie to tell her the plan. Connie agreed, and in fifteen minutes they had picked her up and were on their way to the Boynton farm. Riley was behind the wheel. Trish, not accustomed to traveling on narrow country roads, asked, "Don't you think you ought to slow down a bit?" When they met another vehicle and the tires on the passenger side left the pavement, Trish covered her face and offered a sigh of relief when they were safely back on road. "Maybe you would like for me to drive?" she asked.

They turned into the little road that led to the farmhouse and Riley brought the car to a stop in front of the big wraparound porch. There was a beautiful sunset off to the west, but Riley hardly noticed it as she got out of the car. "Why don't you two stay here, and I'll return as soon as I can," she suggested.

Riley knocked on the door four times, pounding louder with each effort. Finally, the door opened. Mrs. Boynton stood in front of her. Riley could tell by her red eyes that she had been crying. "Wilma," she said. I want to talk with you and Kaylene. Is she home?" It was at that moment that the mother broke into hysterical tears.

CHAPTER 3

Riley helped Wilma to a nearby sofa and sat with her, trying to calm her by putting one arm around her shoulders and taking one of her hands into hers. It was difficult to understand her words because of the crying and whimpering. "They've taken her. They've taken my precious baby."

"Take deep breaths and try to settle down," Riley told her. "We have all the time in the world." After a couple of minutes, the nearly hysterical mother seemed to regain a measure of composure. "Now, can you tell me what's got you so upset? Just take it slow and easy."

Wilma began to cry again. Riley patted her shoulder and whispered, "What happened? Is Kaylene in trouble?"

"I can't tell anyone. They said they'd kill her," Wilma said quietly through her tears.

"Does someone have Kaylene?" Riley prodded. "I'm here to help. You can tell me."

"He said we would never see her again if we told anyone."

"Who told you that?" Riley asked.

"Don't you understand? Some awful person has kidnapped her. We don't know who."

"Does he want money?"

"No, he said nothin' about money. He wants Nate to drop out of the election or we'll never see her again." Wilma started weeping again. "You can't tell this to anyone. If he knows I've told you, he'll kill her."

"I promise you, if it's what you want, I'll tell no one. I love Kaylene too, and I don't want any harm to come to her. When did it happen?"

"It wasn't long after you dropped her off yesterday. She was alone, doin' some work down in the barn, and then we couldn't find her. A few minutes later, Sam got a phone call from some man who told us the only way we could get our little girl back was to get Nate to drop out of the election in the next week."

"Does Nate know about this?" Riley asked.

"Of course he does. I think, maybe, he's going to do what they asked, but we are afraid even then, we may never see our little girl again. We have six more days, but I want her back now."

"Where's Sam?" Riley asked.

"He's over at Nate's place. They're talkin' about what we ought to do. He should be back soon."

"I'll stay with you till he gets back."

They sat on the sofa, mostly silent, Riley with her arm around the desperate mother and Wilma with her head on Riley's shoulder. After a few minutes Sam came through the front door. It was the only time Riley had encountered him when he didn't seem happy to see her. "I thought that was your car," he said to her with a sour expression on his face.

"Hello, Sam. Before you come to any conclusions, let me tell you what's happened here. I came to see Kaylene. It was obvious that Wilma was extremely troubled. She didn't want to tell me anything, but I prodded until I got enough from her to understand that Kaylene has been taken. I promised her I would tell no one, and that means no one. You can count on it."

"I hope so," Sam replied. "Our baby's life may depend on it."

"Have you thought about going to the police?" Riley asked.

"Of course, we thought about it, but we can't do that. Anyone that would go so far as to kidnap a child, probably wouldn't hesitate to take that child's life. They gave us a week. I just talked with Nate again. He's goin' to wait a few days to see what happens. Then if we don't get her back, he'll withdraw."

"It seems to me the only thing you can do is follow whatever instructions you get. I'm going to get out of your way now, but I want you to know you are not in this alone. I'll be praying," Riley told the distressed parents, making eye contact with Sam and then Wilma. She hugged each before leaving. "You know that God's still in charge, don't you? Wilma, let me know if you need to talk. I know it's what people say to friends in distressing times, but I mean it when I say, let me know immediately if there's anything I can do for you."

"You can find my baby and bring her home," Wilma said almost calmly, with deep sadness consuming her face.

"I'm going to try, sweet lady," Riley said to herself as she walked across the front porch and into the yard. "I'm going to do my best to bring her home to you."

Before putting the key in the ignition, Riley turned toward Trish and said, "I can't tell you anything about what's going on here. To do so would be to break a confidence. But there are two brokenhearted parents in that house and a traumatized elderly gentleman in the one next door." She then twisted all the way around to face Connie. "They need our help. Are you with me?' she asked in rather dramatic fashion.

"Just tell me what to do," Connie responded from the back seat.

"I've got a feeling I might regret this later, but I'm with you too," Trish declared.

"Then let's get started," Riley said before starting the engine. "Our first order of business is to take a look at that old house where Amos saw the car speeding away this morning."

"Do we have to do that tonight? It's almost dark out there. Couldn't it wait until morning?" Trish asked.

"Time is not our ally right now," Riley told her as she urgently but cautiously chauffeured them along one of the county's many country roads. "We need to do it now. Connie, you know more about these things than me. Why is the county commissioner's post such a sought-after position?"

"That's an easy question to answer. It's because county commissioner is the most powerful political position in our county. Not much happens around here unless it's approved by the commissioner. Most of the counties in the state have a board of commissioners who make such decisions. We are one of the few that does not. It's all left to that one man. A lot of people like our setup because it tends to speed up projects. Endeavors move much faster when you have only one person to convince rather than several. On the other hand, a lot of people argue that no individual should have that kind of power. It can lead to corruption, they claim. They believe important decisions should be made by multiple people. Sort of a check and balance arrangement, I guess. I can see both sides of the argument. Before takin' the position I now hold with you folks, I leaned toward having a board. Now, I kinda like being able to get quick approvals for some of our plans."

They met a car with its high beams on. Being slightly blinded for a moment, Riley slowed down. "That wasn't a metallic green Kia Soul, was it?" Riley asked.

"No, it wasn't a Kia. I'm not sure what it was, but it definitely wasn't a Kia Soul," Connie answered.

"Are you telling me you couldn't see that car well enough to distinguish it's color?" Trish asked. "I'm nearsighted and I could see that it was white."

"I've got nearly perfect vision, but it's hard to see well when you're looking directly into lights that bright. Don't worry, Trish. I'll get us there safe and sound. Just relax."

"One more thing about our commissioner-versus-board-of-commissioners discussion," Connie said. "The puzzlin' rumors I've heard is that even though he's runnin' for the office, Nate is actually opposed to the single commissioner system. I've been told, if he wins, he'll be workin' toward changin' it. If he gets his way, he'll be the last person to hold the position."

"That's interesting," Riley said. "Sometimes you amaze me. I'm the law student, but I have to look to you to learn about our political system."

"The difference is that you've lived in Georgia and been a weekend resident of Bartow County for only a year. I've been here all my life."

Riley slowed the car to turn into the drive that led to their destination. She turned off the headlights. "What are you doing?" Trish immediately asked.

"I don't think there'll be anyone there since Amos scared them away, but if there is, I don't want them to see us coming." Riley continued to drive slowly until they got to the top of the hill and could faintly see the house in the distance. She killed the engine. "This is where we get out, girls. Don't slam your doors. We don't want anyone to hear us. Bring your phones. We may need them as flashlights."

"Or to call for help," Trish suggested.

They started their hike to the little house in single file with Riley leading the way, Trish second, and Connie bringing up the rear. "What will we do if we find someone in the house?" Trish suddenly asked as they trekked along the drive that was little more than a trail.

Riley didn't answer at first, then quietly responded, "I don't know. We'll figure that out if it happens."

"That's what I like about you, Riley. You always have a plan."

"Okay, we're getting closer. From here on in, we need total silence." They slowed their pace, then almost tiptoed one by one onto the porch. Riley went to the window to the left of the door and looked inside while listening closely to see if she could hear anything. "There doesn't seem to be anyone around. Let's turn on our flashlights and go inside." Riley led the way through the door. She could almost feel Trish breathing down her neck.

Riley first focused on the bags, wrappers, and cups scattered around the front room floor. She leaned over to look at the trash while using her right foot to move some of it about. "It looks like whoever was here stayed for two or three days. There is trash from at least three fast-food places here," she said. "Evidently they prefer variety. There's stuff from McDonald's, Burger King, and Zaxby's. All three of those places are within walking distance from my place."

Connie walked to the other side of the room with her light turned toward the floor. She leaned over and picked up a small object which she examined closely, holding it in her left hand and her flashlight in her right. "Look at this," she called out to her companions. They huddled together with all three lights pointed at Connie's left hand. What they saw was a small lapel pin with a white background, a blue, kite-shaped edge, a blue caduceus, a blue cross, and gold lettering that read *Licensed Vocational Nurse.* "Is this anything important?"

"You bet it is," Riley answered as Connie handed her the pin. She remembered commenting on that pin when Kaylene wore it on her collar to Sunday School, but in keeping with her promise to the Boyntons, she said nothing to the other ladies. The Kid had told her it was a gift from Nate. She had undoubtedly left the pin there while the house was being quickly abandoned to let it be known she had been there. That's good, Riley thought. *She's keeping her wits about her. I would expect nothing less from such a spunky little lady.*

At that moment Riley was startled by a loud scream from one or maybe both of the other girls that almost caused her legs to buckle. She managed to turn her light in the direction Connie and Trish were focused. She gasped when she saw what had prompted the sudden commotion. She could not believe the size of the racoon casually lumbering across the floor toward the door. Being a city girl, Riley had seen few of this species of animal, but this was definitely the biggest she had ever laid eyes on. She backed toward the corner farthest away from the rambling animal with the other two ladies locked on her arms. "If we don't bother him, he won't harm us," Riley said nervously, trying as much to convince herself as her companions. The racoon walked on past them and out the front door. They followed him at a distance as far as the open door. They watched him amble down the porch, across the small yard, and into the field at the side of the house.

"I've got to sit down," Trish said, sounding as if she was out of breath. She found what looked like a clean spot and flopped onto the floor. "My legs won't hold me any longer."

"You sit right there while I go and check out the other three rooms," Riley suggested.

"No way," Trish responded jumping up. "Wherever you go, I go."

The three ladies cautiously searched the other rooms but found no more clues. On their way home, they decided it was too late for them to go to dinner at the Adairsville Inn. They would catch the inn another day and go to Zaxby's tonight. The fast-food establishment would be open until 11 p.m.

When Trish left the table at the restaurant to go to the restroom, Riley hesitantly turned to Connie. "I need a favor, and it's something that would be helpful for me to have immediately. I know you are a genius at researching hard-to-find information. It would sure be useful for me if I had a list of the projects Nate has come out against in his campaign. I could also use a list of all the people who would be affected should he be successful in making those changes. It would also help me greatly if you could list any enemies Nate might have made in recent years."

"Sure, no guarantees, but I'll see what I can do for you. If you don't mind my lettin' some other things slide, I'll try to have that ready for you early tomorrow afternoon."

"As far as I'm concerned, this takes priority. I'll tell Amos that you will spend the morning doing some work for me. I don't think it'll be a problem. I don't usually interfere in your work so surely the guys will allow me this one impropriety. I don't think I have to tell you that this thing we have found ourselves knee-deep in may very well be a matter of life and death."

"I know you can't break your promise and tell me whether I'm right or wrong, but based on what I've heard and observed, I would say the Kid has been kidnapped and is bein' held until Nate pulls out of the election."

"As you said, I can't break my promise, but let me say, you are a very smart lady."

Trish returned to the table. "What's next, general?" she asked before sitting up straight in her chair. "Now that I've gotten some nourishment and taken care of some other private matters, I'm ready to forge ahead."

"We are going home now," Riley declared. "I need to run some things through my mind before doing anything else. We'll get an early start in the morning."

They delivered Connie to her front door. Riley noticed when they drove into her own driveway that lights were still on in the Edwards' living quarters. *Good, they haven't gone to bed yet.* As they were going up the stairs, she gave Trish the keys to her apartment and told her she had to talk with Amos but would be only a few minutes.

She rang the Edwards' doorbell and waited for the door to open. It was Amos who appeared. "Hi, Riley. What can I do for you? Carol has already retired, but I'm at your service. Come on in where we can be comfortable."

"No, I don't want to wake Carol. I can take care of my business right here at the door.

"Is there something wrong?" Amos asked, stepping into the hallway and closing the door behind him. Riley's demeanor seemed more serious than he was accustomed to.

"Well, not everything is exactly right, but I would have to break a confidence to reveal the whole story to you. Even though I would like nothing better than to lay it out for you, unfortunately, I can't. But you can help me. I know a lot of your buddies get around a lot. Would you put the word out for them to keep a lookout for that metallic green Kia you saw this morning at the old house? Also, ask the Cleaning Crew to keep an eye out for the same car at the fast-food restaurants out at the highway. I'm sure there aren't many vehicles that color around here. Tell them that should they spot it, they are not to follow, but try to determine the direction it is traveling and immediately report back to me."

"Sure, I'll take care of it, but I'm worried. All this seems so ominous. I don't want to sound bossy, but I do want to caution you to be careful not to get into somethin' over your head. I would never forgive myself if somethin' happened to you here in our backyard."

"Don't worry, Amos, I'll be alright. It's just something I've got to do. Incidentally, I asked Connie to do some research for me in the morning, if that's okay with you."

"That's fine. It's no problem if you need her all day. This operation is yours, not mine. You and Kirby call the shots."

"Thanks, Amos. You're too good to me. Don't know what I'd do without you."

When she finally got to bed, Riley lay awake asking herself lingering questions. All evening she had made quick decisions. Where those decisions appropriate? Should she have told the Boyntons that Kaylene had been spotted in a metallic green Kia? Was she right in promising them she would stay quiet about the kidnapping and not go to the police? Should she have broken her promise and told Amos the whole story? Should she call Kirby and reveal everything to him? This was his kind of thing. He would know what to do. Every decision she had made that evening was to protect the life of that precious little girl. She would continue to do what she thought best for the Kid. It was past one-thirty before she finally fell asleep.

CHAPTER 4

"**D**on't call me little girl," Kaylene raised her voice to make her point. "My name is Kaylene. Most people call me Kid, but no one calls me little girl. I can drive a tractor, and I can throw a baseball further than most teenaged boys. I'm not a little girl."

"I'll call you whatever I want," the pudgy, middle-aged woman responded. She had a long face that never seemed to smile. "You need to learn to keep your mouth shut, or you'll soon feel the back of my hand across your face."

"You hit me, and you'll have Nate and my daddy to deal with. You're already in big trouble for takin' me and tyin' my hands. This rope is so tight it's cuttin' my wrist. Just wait. I know Charlie Nelson, the Adairsville police chief. He's goin' to catch you and you'll spend a long time in jail. You're not from around here, are you? If you were, you would know you can't get away with this. They'll find you, then it's, 'Katy, bar the door.'"

"Don't you ever stop runnin' your mouth?" the woman asked while reaching for a large black purse, from which she pulled out a green scarf. "You see this? If you don't quiet down, I'm goin' to use it to gag you."

"You just better not hurt me. Where is Houston? Has he gone to get food again? You folks sure eat a lot."

"You don't fret about Houston. He'll be back soon, and if you don't behave yourself, you're in big trouble with him. You don't want to get in trouble with Houston. You've seen that gun he carries."

"Yes, I've seen it, and it doesn't scare me. I bet he doesn't even know how to load it. My daddy taught me how to shoot a rifle and a handgun, and I can probably shoot better than old Houston."

"Oh, he knows how to use it. You may be a good shot, but that doesn't help you if you don't have a gun," the woman declared.

"Why are you stayin' in a place like this? There are plenty of cheap motels around here," Kaylene exclaimed. "Not that it was any better, but why didn't Houston like that old school we stopped at?"

"It's none of your business. But, if it'll keep you quiet, it was because there was no place there to get the car out of sight."

"Why does the car need to be out of sight?"

"That does it." The woman jerked the scarf back out of her purse and rolled it until it was just right for use as a gag. She put it in Kaylene's mouth and tied it in a knot at the back of her head.

The kid silenced, the woman leaned back in the old metal chair she had found earlier. *Why are we staying in a place like this?* She asked herself the same question the girl had asked her. *This ain't what I bargained for when I married up with Houston. It's been nothin' but trouble and hard times. I know he's goin' to murder that little girl. It doesn't matter how annoyin' she is, I don't want her dead.*

After about ten minutes, the quietness was more than the woman could stand. She got up from her chair and went over to the kid. She loosened the knot she had tied in the scarf. Immediately, the kid blurted out, "I knew you really liked me."

"Oh, my word," the woman moaned and briefly considered putting the gag back in place.

***

Riley rose before the sun. She went into her guestroom where Trish was still in deep slumber. "Time to get up, Sleeping Beauty," she said as she put a hand on one of Trish's shoulders to shake her. "We're going out for breakfast."

"Oh, good," Trish responded in a half-awake voice, rubbing her eyes. "Are we going somewhere special?"

"Well, must be. A lot of people go there for breakfast," Riley told her. "We're leaving in ten minutes."

"Ten minutes! That's not enough time to shower and get ready."

"You can do that when we return. Just pull on some clothes and run a brush through your hair. You don't have to dress up for this place."

Riley was not lying when she said lots of people frequented the Adairsville Hardee's for breakfast. She learned several months earlier that a lot of men, most of whom were retired and looking for something resembling a social life, flocked to the fast-food place almost every morning for biscuits and conversation. Today, Riley wanted to be there because from a parking spot on the west side of the establishment, she could see the lots of several fast-food outlets, including McDonald's. She thought there might be a good chance the driver of a certain metallic green Kia Soul might be coming to one of those places for breakfast.

"You're kidding me," Trish said when they pulled into the line for window service. "We got up at the crack of dawn for this?"

"They tell me, best biscuits in town," Riley declared.

They were fortunate to get the perfect parking space. Riley was at the exact angle she needed to see the lots she wanted to keep tabs on.

Trish noticed that as they ate their breakfast out of the bag, Riley's eyes remained focused straight ahead, rarely turning in her direction. A couple got out of a car that parked nearby, then waved and smiled at them. "Is that someone you know?" Trish asked,

"That's Lee and Sherrie Wright. They're part of our church. I love them. They're a fun couple. Lee is Amos's nephew."

"You seem to have a lot of friends from church. It must be a good one," Trish said.

"It's a great church," Riley agreed. "Oh, in a lot of ways, it's a typical small-town church. Our building isn't a cathedral with ivy growing up the outside walls. We don't have the programs that a lot of big city churches have, or the music talent on our worship team that you might find in some other groups. But it's a great church because it's made up of good people who love the Lord and want to serve him. Kirby had gotten away from the Lord, but he spent almost three months here recuperating from the leg wound he received. The people in the church played a big part in helping him heal, both physically and spiritually.

He found a church he likes when he returned to St. Pete, and, thanks to some of his friends there, he has continued his spiritual progress. I believe it's safe to say that he's back. I'm so proud of him."

"That's fantastic. I'm glad for Kirby." Trish paused. "You know, Riley, I don't think you'd be very proud of me if you'd followed me around the last few months. One aspect of our friendship I most valued was your adeptness at helping me grow stronger in the Lord. I loved it when the two of us shared those special times together, like when we were helping with that downtown Boston mission."

"You remember how your folks almost lost it when they learned where we were spending our Tuesday nights?" Riley laughed. "I thought they were going to move you back home."

"But to their credit, they were okay with it after we took them down to the mission that one night and put them to work in the kitchen. I guess they could see it wasn't as dangerous as they had suspected."

"Those were good times," Riley said.

"I'd like to bring back those days. My spiritual life over the last year has been pitiful. I need your help, Riley. I've lost my zeal for the spiritual side of life, and I've lost most of the joy I had when we were serving the Lord together."

"Haven't you been active in your home church?" Riley asked.

"The truth is, I've seldom attended in the past six months, and I don't know if they've even noticed yet. There's just not much going on there. It's the same old routine week after week with the same old people."

"Maybe you're the person to change that," Riley suggested. At that moment Riley was startled by a knock on the glass beside her head. She turned to see a young man in a police uniform standing there with a grin on his face. "We'll talk about this more," she said to Trish before pushing the button to lower the window.

"I've had some complaints about loitering," the policeman said when the window no longer separated him from Riley.

"Don't pay any attention to him, Trish," Riley told her friend. "This is the charming Mike Unger I've been telling you about. Is this where you boys in blue gather for your coffee and donuts in the mornings?"

"Sometimes, when we're on patrol, we stop here to get a cup of coffee," he admitted.

"Mike, this is Trish Banks, my best friend from college. You've heard me speak of some of the adventures I've shared with her."

"I bet she hasn't shared all of them with you." Trish stretched her right arm out in front of Riley to offer her hand to Mike. "It's good to finally get to meet you," she said with her biggest Trish smile.

"What're you ladies doing out so early on a Friday morning?"

"We got hungry for a Hardee's biscuit, and, since it's only a couple of blocks away, here we are."

"Knowing you as I do, I suspect there's more to it," Mike replied. "But I also know that if you don't want to tell me what it's all about, a team of horses couldn't pull it out of you."

"Such a suspicious mind. If I were here to meet some guy, you don't think I would be dressed like this, do you?" Riley held her hands to her side and looked down at her sweatshirt and jeans.

"You're beautiful, no matter what you're wearing. Here comes Tom with the coffee. I better get back to my car. Good to meet you, Trish. You gonna be here for a while?" Mike bent to look past Riley to Trish.

"A few days. I'm not sure exactly when I'll leave."

"Good. Then I'll probably see you again," the young policeman said with a smile as he touched the bill of his cap. "Hope to see you soon too, sweet lady," he said to Riley before walking away from them to join his partner in their patrol car.

"He's cute. If you don't want him, I'll take him," Trish announced.

"I've never said I didn't want him. I'm just not sure he's the one."

"So, you're just holding him in reserve in case someone better doesn't come along?"

"I'm not holding him at all. He's free to do whatever he wants and to see whomever he wants to see. And it's not a matter of better or best.

I don't know that there's anyone better than Mike. I just don't know if he's the right one for me."

"Don't you think you should have told him about why we are actually here this morning?

"What're you talking about, Trish? I told him we're here to eat breakfast and that's what we've been doing."

"I'm not totally dumb, Riley. I don't know the whole story, but I do know we have been sitting here watching the parking lots across the street, probably for a green Kia. You didn't even see Mike coming because your eyes have been fixed in that direction. You've hardly looked at me since we've been here. And I figure it's because someone in that green Kia has that kid. Now, don't you think you should tell Mike and let him do his job?"

"I wish I could, Trish, but I can't tell him or anyone else. I don't want to get anyone killed."

"I don't fully understand, but I know you and trust you. Wherever you lead, I'll tag along.

"Thank you, Trish. You're the best friend I've ever had. You know if it were possible, I would tell you everything."

"I know," Trish replied. "We'd better keep our eyes peeled across the street."

***

Nate Bannister was alone. He couldn't remember the last time he was in such a funk. Perhaps not since Annie, his wife of almost thirty years, had passed. The kid was in deep trouble, and he was to blame. What made him think he could do the work of a county commissioner anyway? He was nothing more than a farmer and a baseball player. He would pull out of the election today if it would bring her home. But he and Stan talked about it, and they concluded he should not hurry his withdrawal.

If the kid could identify the kidnappers, they were not going to release her. Perhaps he needed to wait as long as possible, since the abductors might have decided they needed her alive until they got what they wanted.

None of it made any sense to him. He sometimes thought of himself as a hard old man, but he knew he could never be so heartless as to harm a child. *Who are these people?* He had spent much of the previous night pondering that question, but no name emerged. There was that man in the expensive suit who had argued with him at the candidate's luncheon, but he doubted he was the kind of man who would stoop this low. He also thought about Adam Carson, who owned all that land he wanted to unload on that theme park company. *He certainly wasn't happy when he learned my position on that, but, no, I can't believe he could be behind anything like this.* Maybe if he knew who they were, he could go after them and bring her home. He paced for a while, then sat down in the old brown chair in which he spent most of his time when home. His attention went across the room to a beautifully framed picture of him with four other all-star pitchers. It had been taken at Fenway Park in Boston during the preliminaries of one of the five all-star games in which he had participated. The kid had taken it on herself to get that old photo blown up and framed. She gave it to him on his last birthday. It was one of his most prized possessions. Then he felt tears involuntarily flowing down his cheeks again. It had happened several times since Stan gave him the news. Everywhere he looked there were mementos of his special friendship with the kid.

I've got to do something. I could never forgive myself if anything hap-pened to her. He got out of his chair again, walked a few steps to a small lamp table, and pulled a handgun from the drawer. He put it in the right pocket of his pants. Then he went through the door and headed for his car. *I can't sit here and do nothing.* He wasn't sure what he was looking for, but he knew he had to get out of the house. Maybe he would ac-cidently run upon the kid playing at one of her favorite places. That's what he would do, he decided. He would drive past a few of her favorite hangouts. What else was there to do?

***

Riley and Trish's stakeout of the fast-food parking lots paid no dividends. That concerned Riley. Maybe the kidnappers had left the area, and if so, what had they done with Kaylene? Of course, there were places other than those they were watching where breakfast was available. When they returned home, Trish took possession of the bathroom. Knowing from experience that Trish didn't do brief showers, Riley decided to go downstairs to Kirby's bathroom for her own shower. Afterward, she was back in her sitting room, dressed and ready for the day when Trish would finally return from her own leisurely bath.

"Well, what do we do next, captain?" Trish asked when she emerged.

"You've demoted me. Yesterday I was a general."

"It doesn't matter. I'm a private and even a corporal outranks me. You're still in charge."

"I was just pondering where we might go from here. I've got to meet with Connie in the early afternoon. Hopefully she'll have the results of some research she's doing for me. Maybe that'll help us to decide what's next."

"I know better than to ask the nature of the research," Trish moaned.

"Sorry. You know I would tell you if I could."

Riley's phone rang. "Riley this is Amos. I thought you would want to know that when I asked Blake Gardner to keep an eye out for that metallic green Kia, he told me he saw one yesterday. He was on his way to North Rome to take care of someone's air conditioner unit when he passed the old model school buildin' in Shannon. He said it was because of the color that he noticed the car sittin' between the two buildings."

"I know where you're talking about, Amos. It's the remains of the vacated school on the right side of the Old Rome Calhoun Highway."

"That's it," Amos assured her. "But you're not goin' there alone. I'd be happy to drive over there with you."

"No reason for that. Trish will keep me company. Looking forward to having dinner with you and Carol tonight. Talk with you then. Bye."
Riley turned her phone off before Amos could further state his case for going along. It might be beneficial to have him with them, but she didn't

want to be pressed into giving him an explanation of the reason for the short journey.

"I assume we're off again," Trish said, rising from the sofa and reaching for her fashionable brown bag.

"Just a short trip to Shannon," Riley told her.

"A lovely name for a town. Sounds Irish."

"Actually, it's an old north Georgia mill village."

CHAPTER 5

"I've heard people speak of mill villages, but I don't have the slightest idea what the term means," Trish admitted as Riley navigated through the road construction on the way to Shannon.

"There are remnants of several mill villages around north Georgia. Shannon is probably one of the more intact examples, though the community is no longer the property of the mill. In fact, some years ago the textile mill closed after running three round-the-clock shifts for decades. I believe, in the beginning, it was Brighton Mills. Back in the early to mid-twentieth century it was one of the major industries in this area. Hundreds of people worked in the mill, lived in the company houses, shopped in the company store, worshipped in the company churches, played in the company park, socialized in the company hall, and swam in the company pool. It was a culture all its own." Riley saw a man up ahead wearing a construction hardhat and holding a red flag and she gradually brought her Ford to a standstill. "It's a little inconvenient to travel through here now. As you can see, they're converting the highway to four lanes."

"Shannon seems to be a relatively pleasant place to live for those not blessed with a lot of income," Riley continued her conversation about their destination. "A couple of families who attend our church live there. There's a nice county park at the site of the old company park. It has a walking track, playground, meeting hall, ballparks, paved basketball court, frisbee course, and such. I think it's well used by people from the region."

"And what about our immediate destination—the abandoned school? What's it's story?" Trish asked.

"Model schools, consisting of elementary, middle, and high school, once stood about a half mile from the main part of the village. The complex was relocated thirty or forty years ago to another location several miles down the road. Part of the old complex has been used by a small manufacturing company, but some of it was demolished. Three or four of the old buildings still stand but are in rather pathetic condition. A while back I read online that those buildings are haunted. I don't know the story behind the alleged ghost, but I guess it's supposed to be some high school student who died there in an accident. Reports have been given of small glittering lights being seen through the windows on certain nights."

"Don't tell me that," Trish whined. "At least we'll be there in the daytime. I can deal with ghosts during the day, but don't want anything to do with them after dark."

"Dead people can't harm us. It's those who're alive that we need to be on the lookout for," Riley stated. "If we do see anyone there, we need to stay completely out of sight. It could be a matter of life or death for a precious little girl."

After a few minutes, pointing to the right, Trish asked, "Is that it?"

"That's it," Riley confirmed as she turned right and drove a few hundred yards before whipping into a drive behind what looked like the best preserved of the remaining buildings. She proceeded to circle the run-down complex. "There's no place anyone could hide a car here. Looks like they're not here. I don't know if I'm relieved or disappointed." When they got back to the place where they started their loop, she stopped the car, killed the engine, and opened the door.

"We're not going inside those buildings, are we?" Trish asked with a voice that almost seemed to quiver.

"You can remain here if you'd like," Riley told her. "I'm going to see if there is any way of getting in so I can look around."

"Didn't you see that No Trespassing sign in front of the building?"

"I did, and it may be wrong for me to ignore it, but sometimes you just have to do what must be done."

"Okay, wait for me, I'm right behind you. Do you think Amos will bail us out?" Trish asked.

Riley, already climbing the back steps, ignored her. Even before she got to the door, she saw that someone had probably used a wedge of some kind to work on the chain and padlock that had once secured the entrance. She pulled the door, and it opened. Trish followed close behind her as they walked down the hallway where long ago boisterous high school students had hurried to the next class. "What are we looking for? Trish asked.

"I don't know, exactly. I guess any sign that someone might have been here in the last day or two."

Most of the classroom doors were closed, but Riley quickly discovered they weren't locked. The young women cautiously peeped into each room. Some were almost empty. A few held antique desks and old school equipment. Others were cluttered with nothing but trash, but there was no sign of anyone having hidden there. Riley was too concerned about the possibility of rats and snakes to scratch around in the rooms too much. With rooms on both sides of the hallway and doors mostly closed, there wasn't much light in the hallway. Riley suggested they turn around to exit the same way they came in. Trish breathed a sigh of relief.

They tried the doors of two other buildings, but discovered they were locked. Before they got back to their vehicle, a Floyd County police cruiser drove by. There were two officers in the car. The one in the passenger seat turned to look their way as they passed. He continued to stare until they were out of sight.

"Uh oh," Trish said. "I hope you've got Amos's number or, better yet, the number of a good bail bondsmen."

"If they return, let me do the talking. You just sit in the car and stay silent," Riley instructed her panicky partner. They both got into the car expecting the cruiser to pull in at any minute, but it never happened. "We got lucky," Riley declared with relief.

Trish laid her head back on the headrest and put her right hand on her heart. "My mom would've had a heart attack had she received word that I was wearing stripes in a southern jail."

"I was going to show you the village, but I think maybe we ought to make a beeline for Adairsville," Riley declared, already moving in that direction. She said nothing to Trish, but she was relieved when they crossed back into Bartow County.

***

Riley left Trish doing her nails at the apartment while she went to see Connie at her office. She was pleased to get the opportunity to chat on the sidewalk with Davis and Deidre Morgan and their little son. Davis, the proprietor of the Corra Harris bookstore, one of several businesses in the 1902 Stock Exchange down the street, had quite a reputation as a detective. She was always amazed at how well Davis maneuvered on his crutches. She wished she could talk with him about the situation in which she currently found herself, but she knew she didn't dare. "We'll see you tonight," Deidre told her. "Amos and Carol invited us for dinner, and I understand you'll be there."

"I can't wait. My friend Trish will be there also. You'll enjoy meeting her," she called back as she started her climb up the stairs to the office.

As Riley knew she would, Connie had a small stack of material for her. Riley sat in a chair in front of the desk while Connie began her explanation of what she had found. "These are the proposed projects Nate has come out against. I've put together as much information as I could locate about the details of each. You'll find names and information about the people behind the projects, as well as the identity of people in the community who are likely to benefit from them. I have also included profiles of a couple of people who've gone head-to-head with Nate about matters not related to the commissioner's post. I hope you'll find somethin' here that'll be of help. Are you makin' any progress?" she asked.

"I'm afraid the answer is no," Riley answered, dropping her head. "We're working on it, but mostly spinning our wheels."

"I know you well enough to know you're not goin' to get discouraged and give up."

"No, we can't afford to do that, but it's so frustrating. There're so many people whose help I could use, but this confidentiality thing has me all tied up. I just saw Davis. He would be on this like a bloodhound after a fugitive if he only knew. And Chief Charley Nelson ought to be leading this investigation. Maybe even the FBI, but I can't tell anyone."

"Well, you know I'm ready to help. Just say the word, and I'll be there."

"I know that. Maybe your research will give us a clue."

"I'll see you tonight at Amos and Carol's little get together. They invited both mom and me."

"Great," Riley replied with a smile. *I didn't know this event was going to be a full-scale dinner party.*

***

First chance I get I'm out of here, the Kid told herself. *It's probably ten or twelve miles home once I get outside this buildin', and my hands are tied, but that doesn't matter. I'm gone if I get the opportunity.* It crossed her mind that now might be the time. Houston and the woman were probably at least seventy feet away. She could start running in the opposite direction. She was sure she could outrun and outlast both Houston and the woman, but she didn't know if there was a means of escape from the big building down there. The only way of entering and exiting she knew about was the one they used when they entered, and it was on the other side of her captors. *Better wait until I can get a good lead going in that direction.*

Both the man and woman glanced her way regularly as they talked. It looked as if they were arguing about something. Kaylene couldn't pick up on what they were saying, but she could see that their conversation was heated. Occasionally she could hear Houston raise his voice, though she could not understand his words. Not only was the distance a deterrent, but they didn't talk like her. They spoke with an accent. She had already learned that Houston did not like to miss a meal. They were not near any fast-food place that she could remember. He would be gone to get supper for at least half an hour. That was probably when she should make her move. *I can run past the woman and get to the door before she gets started good.*

The Kid tried to get comfortable in her little nest on the floor, but with her hands tied behind her she had to lie on her side or stomach which made it difficult. The more she thought about her plan, the more confident she became. She knew her parents and Nate would be searching for her but doubted they would find her in this big ole deserted factory building. She would have to do it herself. The only thing that concerned her was Houston's gun. He had left it with the woman only once when he had gone for food. She would have to think about whether or not to make her move if the woman had the gun. She didn't think she would shoot her, and, even if she did pull the trigger, she doubted she was much of a shot.

***

Amos and Carol loved people. The evening that began in their apartment before spreading into the garden reflected that. Connie and her mother, Beth Reece, were there, as were Davis and Deidre Morgan. Riley was disappointed that their little son, Charles, had been left with a babysitter. Mike Unger and a friend of his, Nathan Bailey, had also been invited, although they arrived a little later than the other guests. Mike said something about having to stay on duty a little longer than his schedule called for. Riley guessed Amos or Carol had invited Nathan, hoping he and Trish might hit it off. They soon learned that he had recently accepted the youth pastorate position at the church in Calhoun that Mike attended.

There was one other gentleman there that Riley did not recognize. He was a handsome, well-dressed man with salt-and-pepper hair who seemed very much at home in the midst of a group of strangers. "This is Jason Purcell of Macon," Amos said, introducing Riley to the stranger. "I met him this afternoon. He represents the Outdoor Sportsman, a chain of stores that caters to the outdoorsman. He is in town looking for property for their new store and seems to be interested in a large track of that acreage out on the east side of Highway 75. I told him he would need to speak to you and Kirby, and that it wouldn't be possible for a couple of weeks. He insisted on meeting you anyway, so I invited him to tonight's shindig."

Purcell smiled in Riley's direction. "I appreciate the Edward's allowing me, a stranger, to barge in on their party. It's another example of Adairsville hospitality. It's good to make your acquaintance, Miss Gordan."

"Good to meet you, Mr. Purcell. Perhaps after dinner we can talk, but you need to know that there are four of us who work together in making major decisions. I'm the least involved in matters of business. My brother Kirby, Amos, and Connie, who is sitting over there on the sofa with her mother, are the other members of the team. Enjoy your dinner, Mr. Purcell. Amos and Carol always provide some of the most delightful southern cooking ever put on a table."

"Thank you kind lady. I will look forward to our meeting after dinner."

It was a pleasant evening that afforded Riley the opportunity to visit with Mike. Trish and Nathan seemed to enjoy one another's company. The food could not have been better. Riley especially enjoyed Amos's home-smoked pork barbeque and the blackberry cobbler Carol made for dessert. With Trish in the house, she had skipped her daily running routine the last two mornings, but she knew after tonight she must resume her normal morning schedule.

The highlight of the evening was when Deidre Morgan announced to her friends that her husband had recently walked the entire fourteen feet across a room without his crutches. The bullet of a revengeful escapee had pierced his back a couple of years earlier, causing his doctors to believe he would never walk again. Davis, a man of faith, refused to accept that diagnosis. Day after day, he persisted in every exercise prescribed to him. He knew someday he would be able to get around without the aid of crutches, which he actually used amazingly well. "He's still got a long way to go before we throw those crutches away," Deidre told them. "But he's on his way."

Riley was elated for Davis's progress. He had become one of her and Kirby's most treasured friends and advisors over the past year, and they had grown to love this man and his little family. She credited much of Kirby's spiritual progress to Amos and this quiet, but dynamic, former pastor turned bookseller and police chaplain.

As the hour of nine o'clock drew near, Riley suggested to Amos and Connie that they go with her, along with Mr. Purcell, to her apartment where they could hear what he had to say.

When the little group were all seated, Riley spoke to their guest. "As I told you earlier, no decision is possible without the presence of my brother, but we are happy to hear what you have to say."

"Since we are not all here, I'll be brief. As I have already advised you, we are interested in opening one of our stores in this vicinity. This location would put it exactly halfway between Atlanta and Chattanooga, sixty miles each way. There are other good-sized towns nearby, such as Rome and Cartersville. Those towns appear to be home to a lot of outdoorsmen. Then there are at least three large lakes not far from here that support a lot of fishing and boating. It would seem to be an ideal place for one of our stores, but, of course, it would need to be in close proximity to an interstate highway, and near a ramp. Your property meets that requirement. We would need to have at least thirty acres, but, if the price is right, we might be willing to purchase the entire one hundred and twenty acres. We would like to make you an offer, but there is one condition."

"And what is that condition?" Amos was quick to ask.

"We would want to have a clear go-ahead to put our store on the property before we purchase the property. It is our understanding that one of the candidates for County Commissioner opposes our project, an old ballplayer by the name of Bannister, I believe. My people would probably back-off should he be elected."

Riley and Connie looked at each other.

"You realize we are probably talking about an offer that would be in the millions," Purcell stated. "Our businesses are more than just stores. They provide an experience. This, without doubt, would give a huge shot in the arm to your community's economy. I would recommend that if you have any pull in this county, you do everything you can to keep that old man out of office."

"Mr. Purcell, Nate Bannister is a longtime friend of mine. I could never campaign against him. He's a good man who loves the people in this community," Amos countered.

"Just remember that it could be very costly to you people, should he come out on top."

"I think we've heard enough, Mr. Purcell. Amos, will you show the gentleman out," Riley suggested. "If you wish, you may contact my brother when he returns to town."

Purcell shook hands all around the room before leaving with Amos at his side. "Did you hear anything that sounded suspicious?" Riley asked when they were gone.

"I wouldn't trust him as far as I could throw him," Connie replied. "But if he's on the level, it could certainly be a bonanza for you and Kirby."

"And, no doubt, a big bonus for you and Amos."

CHAPTER 6

I was hoping he would take the gun with him, Kaylene thought as Houston handed the weapon to the woman and started his walk out of the big building.

"I'll be back with dinner in a few minutes," he told his companion.

"Get me somethin' besides a burger," the woman called out to him. "I'm tired of burgers."

"You're lucky to get anything. You'll eat whatever I bring you," Houston told the woman, looking back at her as he walked away.

Kaylene knew she would need to give him enough time to get outside the building and into that ugly green Kia. She didn't want to sprint down the long corridor and through the door only to run into him. The gun was lying on an old homemade table. The woman had her head in the magazine she was holding. Kaylene waited until she thought at least ten minutes had passed, then she jumped to her feet and ran. The woman did not realize what was happening until Kaylene was well past her. Stunned, she reached for the gun only to knock it off the table onto the floor. She dropped to her knees and fumbled for it.

"Stop or I'll shoot you down," the woman shouted.

The Kid kept running. She seemed to pick up speed with each stride. Then she heard a gunshot and a noise sounding like something falling from the ceiling. That told her the woman had fired a shot upward rather than at her. She also figured she had now put enough distance between her and the woman. There was absolutely no way she could target her at that distance, even if she tried. She was home free if only Houston had not locked the door from the outside. She could hear the woman running behind her, shouting for her to stop. She had no intention of stopping. When she came to the door that was the gateway to her freedom, she kicked it hard with her right foot. It opened. *Thank goodness, it isn't locked!*

Now she was outside, still running with a lot of distance between her and the woman. She was glad to see that darkness had already fallen. The woman wouldn't see her in the dark.

Then she came to the fence that reached around the old factory building. She couldn't locate the opening through which they had entered. The chain link fence appeared about seven feet tall with two strands of barbed wire stretched across the top. Being a farm girl, barbed wire didn't bother her a great deal. She might get a few scratches and small cuts, but she had experienced that before. The catch would be climbing the fence with her hands tied behind her. She tried to separate them, hoping to break the knots, but the rope didn't give. She looked first to her right and saw no openings. And then she glanced to her left. It looked like a small hole at the bottom of the fence about fifteen feet from where she now stood. She might be able to squeeze through.

She headed for that break. Laying on her stomach, she managed to slither through the small hole. She then scampered to her feet and scurried a hundred yards or so to the west before turning to her right. The challenge then was to cover the length of the massive manufacturing facility. She knew the woman had probably not gotten past the fence. She turned right and, becoming winded, slowed to a trot as she went past the front of the former company store. Her next move was to head to the sidewalk beside the little road running between the complex and the park. Then only another hundred and fifty yards to cross Highway 53. She would go across the highway and try to get some help from someone at one of the two gas stations on the other side of the heavily traveled throughfare.

She saw both at almost the same time while waiting for traffic to pass. First there was the Subway sign. She had forgotten about the Subway sandwich shop located inside the service station. Then she saw the green Kia coming toward her. Houston had not traveled to Adairsville or Rome for their food. He had gone to Subway. She turned back the way she had come, hoping to find a hiding place before the man saw her, but it was too late. Houston pulled his Kia to the side of the road and in a moment had his grubby arms around her, dragging her kicking and screaming to the car. Kaylene's one hope was that perhaps someone spotted the struggle and would report it.

***

Riley got out of bed before dawn on Saturday morning. She had her quiet time, reading from Proverbs and the book of James. She spent much of her prayer time lifting up Kaylene, her family, and Nate. It was hard for her to think of anything else. She wanted, so much, to help her little friend and those who loved her, but she felt so helpless. While she was waiting for Trish to get up, she took the material Connie had given her to her kitchen table to scan.

Connie's research showed that, indeed, Nate strongly opposed the Outdoor Sportsman coming to Adairsville. Connie had included a short profile of Jason Purcell as well as two other company executives. Riley's brief encounter with Purcell had left her with a rather sour taste, but she could not imagine a reputable company such as his being involved in something like kidnapping.

Nate had also spoken out against the possibility of an amusement park being located south of Adairsville. An investment group was looking into the possibility of a four-hundred-unit apartment complex. Nate felt Adairsville's infrastructure would not support it. Connie had given her plenty of information on those projects and the people pushing them. She was most interested in the people on this end who would benefit most from such ventures—like those who owned the land and those scheduled to do the construction. That information was part of Connie's report. Riley would study it more closely later.

Her eyes were then drawn to a page that revealed two incidents from Nate's earlier life in which he had significant clashes with Adairsville residents. *Where does Connie get this stuff? She's amazing.* Forty years earlier Nate was involved in an automobile accident in which Donald Neff had been seriously injured. Even though Nate was vindicated, Neff felt the verdict was the result of the baseball player's celebrity status. Neff never fully recovered from the injury and never stopped blaming Nate. He died twenty years back, but his son Edward continued to play the blame Nate game. This was worth looking into, Riley decided, noticing that Edward Neff still operated a service station and convenience store near the I-75 ramp. Connie described him as a serious fitness buff and antique collector.

The other incident, which went back twenty-six years, was even more bizarre. Kenneth Cotes, who would now be sixty-five to seventy years of age, found his favorite bird dog in a field with a bullet through its head. Cotes was convinced that because Nate had been seen hunting in the area, he was the guilty party. Nate denied having anything to do with the dog's death, but Cotes never stopped telling people that Nate killed his dog, and he would someday get even. According to Connie, Cotes owned a construction company that was mostly managed by his three sons and was part owner of a fitness gym and restaurant, both in Cartersville.

There was also a profile of Nate's opponent for the commissioner's post. Riley only glanced at it. She had briefly met the man: he was definitely a politician, but not a thug. She had come away believing he was a good man with an overabundance of ambition.

Riley restacked the papers and picked up her phone. She called a mutual friend to get Wilma Boynton's number, then called Kaylene's mother. "Wilma, this is Riley Gordan. I was wondering if you've heard anything from Kaylene?"

"Well, we got a call from that man again. He told us we only had five days left. Nate was here and insisted on talkin' with him. He told the man that he was goin' to have to prove Kaylene was okay before he would do anything. He let her talk for only a few seconds. She said she was fine. Nate told him he would withdraw from the election on Tuesday, but only if Kaylene is allowed to talk to them again that morning."

"At least we know she's okay. That's what's most important. Please know you are constantly in my prayers. Have you been able to come up with any ideas about who has her?" Riley asked.

"No, we don't have a clue. But if we did, there's nothing we could do. I would be afraid to go after her. He might . . ." Wilma couldn't go on. Riley could hear her weeping.

"Please call me if there's any news," Riley requested.

Riley got into her running clothes. No doubt she would have time to do at least three miles before Trish got up.

***

As Riley ran past a convenience store, it suddenly dawned on her that this was Edward Neff's business, the son of the man who feuded with Nate for years about injuries he received in an accident. *Could this be the man behind the Boynton's trouble?* It was a long shot, but she wondered all the same. Connie's report did say the son had continued the incessant finger-pointing. He surely did not want Nate to be county commissioner. She ran another mile before turning around to return home. Her curiosity got the best of her when she approached the store again. What kind of man was Edward Neff? She ran into the parking lot before stopping to catch her breath. She then went inside to the candy counter, where she picked up a Reese's peanut butter cup and took it to checkout. When she saw the charge on the small screen, she took a five-dollar bill from the secret pocket in her running pants and paid the man behind the counter. "Are you Mr. Neff?" she asked the clerk when he handed her the change.

"Yes, I am," the man answered. "I'm Edward Neff."

"I'm Riley Gordan. James Gordan was my uncle," she told him as she extended her hand to shake his. "I often run past here on my daily runs. I guess you have lived here most your life," she speculated while smiling and making eye contact.

"I've lived here all my life," he said. "I've seen you run past. I heard you and your brother inherited your uncle's estate."

"Did you know my uncle?" Riley asked.

"He was a friend of my father. I didn't know him well, but our paths crossed occasionally."

"I'm new to Adairsville and don't know a lot of people. Having lived here all your life, I bet you know everyone?"

"Just about, but a lot of new people have moved here in recent years. It's not like it used to be."

"Maybe you can help me. My brother and I, thanks to my uncle, own some property here as well as a couple of businesses. We're concerned about the county commissioner election coming up. Do you know the two men who are running for that post? Who would you recommend?"

"I have no reservations whatsoever about telling you to vote for Randy Tate. He's an intelligent leader who can do some good things for our community. Bannister, on the other hand, is a senile old baseball player who I wouldn't vote for if he were running for dog catcher. He's dishonest and out for himself. There's not an honest bone in his body."

"Well, you've answered my question," Riley responded. "Thank you, sir, for your candidness. I seldom meet people unafraid to speak their convictions."

"Come back often," Neff called out as she turned to exit. *I don't know if he had anything to do with Kaylene's abduction, but Connie's research was right on the money. He doesn't much like Nate.* She walked around the corner where Neff could not see her and she dropped the candy bar into a waste basket. *I love these things, but I don't need to be eating them.*

Riley was surprised when she returned home to find Trish up and already dressed, sitting on the sofa with a cup of coffee in her hand. She quickly took her own shower and returned to the sitting room to sip coffee with her friend. "Maybe I should have gotten you up to run with me," Riley commented.

"Not unless you wanted to drag me back here after about a half mile. I think that would be my limit. I don't mind working out a little on the equipment in the gym but running is one of life's most dreadful tortures. I don't think God designed us to move beyond a brisk walk."

"I've been thinking about what you told me yesterday about your spiritual life. I remember when we were in college, we both used to have our quiet time. A daily time of quiet fellowship with God in his Word with prayer has continued to be important to me. I get away from that for a couple of days and I find myself slipping. What about you, Trish? Have you continued to schedule such a time?"

"I'm sorry to say that I haven't done that regularly since I returned home from college. I think the problem is no longer having you around to gently nudge me. I have found myself gradually abandoning a lot of the good habits you helped to instill into my life. I think I saw the person you are, and I wanted to be like you. I knew it was your relationship with the Lord that made you different than a lot of others. That motivated me to seek after what you had. I haven't had that since we've been separated."

"Please take me off that pedestal, Trish. I don't belong there. I'm far from being the example God wants me to be. The difference is that I've always had that kind of influence. Currently, it's Amos and Carol who inspire me. Their sweet spirits and total dedication to God make me want to be more than what I am. But I know what you're saying. We all need a mentor. We need someone to be accountable to. I told you that Kirby had backslidden. I think the same thing that happened to you, happened to him. He found himself without a mentor, someone to look up to and be accountable to. After coming here, he found Amos and Davis. It changed his life. When he returned to St. Petersburg, he made sure he found people that could help him continue what had started. That's what you need, Trish. When you return home, you must find that person or persons that will encourage you and motivate you to live for Jesus."

Trish dropped her head to look downward. Before she could speak, Riley's phone rang. "I guess I ought to get that," she said before picking up the sometimes irritating instrument. Riley smiled when she heard Mike's voice.

"I've got a great idea," Mike's tone revealed his excitement. "I've already talked with Nathan about it. Why don't you and Trish drive to Calhoun tomorrow after church and meet us for a drive to Fort Mountain. I'll bring food and we can have a picnic. It might make us a little late getting lunch, but not much. What do you think? Are you game?"

There was a moment of silence. Riley really wanted to accept Mike's invitation. So far, she had been lax in showing Trish a good time. But there was this thing with Kaylene and not much time left. However, unless something came up, she didn't know of anything that would require her time tomorrow. But how could she go out and enjoy herself when Kaylene was going through who knew what? She covered the phone with one hand and asked Trish, "What do you say? Want to go on a picnic tomorrow with Mike and Nathan?"

"You bet I do," Trish responded without hesitation.

"We'll plan to meet you in the church parking lot about twelve-forty-five," she said. "Unless something comes up."

"What could possibly come up? Remember, I'm providing the lunch with picnic basket and the whole bit. Get ready to chow down on some of the best victuals you've ever put into your mouth. The weather is supposed to be good. We'll show your friend a great time. How does she feel about the mountains?" he asked.

"I don't know, but we'll find out tomorrow." Before Riley discontinued the call with the words, "Stay safe," the ladies heard a scratching sound on the door that led to the hallway.

"What's that?" Trish quickly asked.

"That, my friend, is Max."

"Who is Max?"

"I can't believe you've been here a couple of days and haven't yet met Max." Riley walked to the door and opened it. A big, golden colored cat pranced through the doorway. He stood beside Riley's favorite chair until she was seated. Then he jumped into her lap. "This is Max. Max lives with Amos and Carol, but he likes to come here for a visit from time to time."

CHAPTER 7

Nate sat behind the wheel of his three-year-old Chevrolet, parked on a hill beside the road. The rise overlooked the rustic weekend getaway of Kenneth Cotes. Nate was trying to convince himself this was the place he needed to be. *He's the only one I can think of who is low enough to pull something like this. He's hated me ever since someone shot his dog, and I hear he's slated to be the contractor for that large apartment complex I oppose. That gives him double motivation. He wouldn't dare take her to his primary residence. This must be the place, if he has her.* Nate was tempted to drive within five feet of the front door, kick the door open, and storm the cabin with gun in hand. But he dared not do anything that would threaten Kaylene's life. He saw no car in the yard, though one possibly could be hidden behind the log house. He had been on the hill for more than half an hour but had seen no one.

Nate's mind was on the Kid as he waited. She was a livewire for sure. From the time she was nine or ten years old, she had been doing more than her share on the farm. Her two older brothers did what was required of them, but their hearts weren't in it. Now that they were young men, they had moved on to vocations more to their liking. Ella, Kaylene's older sister, had always been more domestic-minded. She liked to do her work inside, but the Kid loved everything about the outdoors. He could barely stand the thought of her bound up somewhere, maybe in a cellar or a small dingy room. Sometimes she irritated the life out of him with her incessant yakking, and sometimes she made him laugh like no one else could. She spoke often of becoming a nurse. He would make sure she had opportunity to realize that dream. He also hoped he lived long enough to someday see her wed the right young man. He would help them get off to a good start financially. But before anything else, she would need to be brought home safely. He would do whatever he had to do to make that happen.

Nate heard something. He glanced into the rearview mirror to see a Bartow County sheriff's cruiser pull in behind him. He pushed the button to lower the window. "Can I help you officer?" he asked, unruffled.

"Yes sir, we saw you sitting here and thought you might need some help."

"No trouble. Just enjoying the view on this beautiful Saturday afternoon," Nate replied.

"You're Nate Bannister, aren't you?" the officer asked excitedly.

"Guilty as charged," Nate responded. "Am I in trouble?"

"No sir," the deputy answered. "When I was a boy, I saw you pitch against the Braves in Atlanta. You blew them away that day. But, of course, in those years everyone seemed to beat up on them."

"Even the worst major league teams are still major league teams. I'm glad you saw one of my good games. I occasionally had a bad one, you know."

"As I understand, not a lot of them," the officer replied with a smile. His eyes went to the seat next to Nate. He saw the .38 lying there. "Do you have a permit for that weapon?" The tone of the policeman's voice was suddenly serious.

"Yes sir. I do." Nate took the license from his billfold and handed it to the officer.

He looked at the small slip of paper and handed it back to Nate. "If I were you, I'd put the gun somewhere out of sight, like in the glove compartment. It would also be best for you to move on to another place for your sightseeing. This is sort of a dangerous place to be parked," he said, maintaining eye contact. "Have a good day sir." He turned to go back to his car.

Nate watched in his rearview mirror as the officer talked to his partner. He was still talking when Nate drove away. *I can't do the Kid any good in jail*, he decided as he drove down past the cabin and out of the sight of the officers.

**

Riley and Trish were looking at a picture album Trish had brought with her. It was an opportunity to relive their college years. "I can't believe I looked like that. Look how long my hair was in those days! And that silly smile on my face," Riley laughed.

"Here's one of you and my mom. Remember that? She came to visit for the day and stayed a week," Trish remarked. "She still does that, you know. She clings to me like I'm her rediscovered lost puppy dog. I think she would go along on my dates if I didn't put my foot down."

"Don't be too hard on her. She's that way because she loves you."

"I just wish she didn't love me so much!"

"Don't say that, Trish. I would give anything to have my mother follow me around for a while."

"I'm sorry, Riley. You know me, old motormouth Banks. I put my foot in my mouth about one out of every two times I open it. I know you must still miss her a lot. How long has it been since you lost your parents?"

"The fifth anniversary of the crash was last Monday. A day hasn't passed since that I haven't thought about them. Sometimes when I hear a mother call to her child, I find myself turning around to answer. A couple of weeks ago, at Emory, I caught a glimpse of a man in a suit and tie disappearing around a corner, and I almost called out to him to wait for me. I keep pictures of them on my computer, and I look at them almost every day. I guess I think I'm going to forget what they look like, and I couldn't bear to do that. Just after the accident happened, a lot of people told me it would get easier in time. It's been five years, and I'm still waiting for it to get easier." Riley barely managed to get the last few words out. There was silence for a minute before she continued. "Life goes on, and I've managed to stay occupied. In a lot of ways, I'm an extremely blessed girl. I've got good friends. I'm doing what I want to do. I have a great brother, and more money than I ever thought possible, but I sure do miss Mom and Dad."

Trish reached across the picture album now lying on the sofa between them and embraced her friend. "I'm ashamed of myself for ignoring your hurt, Riley. I suppose it's because you lost your parents before I knew you, but I've just never given much thought to the grief you must have gone through. Beautiful, strong, and gracious Riley, always first in line to help and encourage everyone else, while hiding your own pain."

"I don't want to make a big deal out of it, Trish. I'm glad we talked, but it does no good to dwell on it. Mom and Dad are in a far better place than any of us, and someday I'll see them again. In the meantime, I have a life—a good life. They made sure of that."

***

Riley walked down the hallway to check in with Amos about what she called an incidental business issue. Trish was left with her thoughts about her heart-to-heart talk with Riley. She never dreamed the perpetually cheerful Riley carried such deep grief. She was the original Suzie Sunshine to most of their college friends. She was the gal who could make the worst disaster seem like Christmas.

Trish wondered if unresolved grief had hindered Riley's love life. The girl had more suitors in college than anyone else she knew. There was no shortage of attention from the opposite sex, and often it came from the most sought-after guys on campus. But three or four dates and Riley usually lost interest. *Mike seems to adore her, but she keeps backing off. Maybe it's "the people I love leave me, and it hurts" syndrome. "If I love him and lose him, it will hurt more than I can bear. So, I won't love him."* That would sure explain a lot. Worth thinking about. Trish wanted to help her most cherished friend but wasn't sure how to go about it. *I wish I had paid more attention to those lectures on grief in psychology class. All that stuff I thought I would never use keeps popping up.* Trish retrieved her laptop and googled "grief." Maybe she could find something that would help her know if her diagnosis was correct. She clicked on several articles but didn't immediately see anything she thought applied to

Riley's situation. After a brief time, she closed her computer, deciding she would resume the search later. *I'm probably overreacting anyway*, she told herself.

Of more immediate concern was Riley's current project. She had pieced together enough to know that a little farm girl was missing, perhaps even kidnapped. She suspected it was a dangerous situation. That concerned her, but Riley had always been there for her. She could think of things she would rather do than search old buildings and stake out parking lots, but there were few activities better than hanging with her best friend, regardless of what they were doing. No, she could not desert Riley. She would see it through. *How dangerous could it be? This isn't the slums of a large city. This is little Adairsville, Georgia.*

Her thoughts went to tomorrow. *What fun it will be to double date with Riley.* They had done that in college. Even when the guys turned out to be duds, it was still enjoyable. And she didn't think Nathan was a dud. She was anxious to get to know him better. She loved his brown eyes and ready smile. She also liked the fact he was a youth pastor. It would be a good day.

***

Riley returned from her session with Amos wearing a big smile on her face. "I've got a surprise for you," she told Trish. "We're going to take a helicopter ride. Amos made all the arrangements with a friend of his at the little airport in Calhoun. We are to meet him there in an hour. Amos is going with us and so is Connie. It should be a lot of fun."

"I don't know about that," Trish was quick to respond. "I've never been in a helicopter before."

"Neither have I or Connie. It'll be a new experience for all of us. You like new adventures, don't you?"

"I like new adventures that allow me to keep both feet on the ground. Can't we just drive around?"

"Okay, you stay here. Connie and I will go. You'll regret it when we come back all excited about how much fun we had."

There was a brief silence. "Fine, I'll go, but you'll be sorry if I have a heart attack or something. What does one wear to ride in a helicopter, anyway?"

"What you have on will be just right. We need to pick up Connie and be on our way," Riley told her.

They met Moncrief Adams, their pilot, shortly after arriving at the airport. "Amos didn't tell me I would have the pleasure of chauffeuring three such beautiful ladies. I understand you want to see Adairsville and it's immediate surroundings from the air," he said.

Adams helped the ladies on board. Amos sat in the seat beside him. Before starting their ascent, the pilot announced, "Fasten your seat belts. In case you were wondering, this is a five-year-old Airbus, model H125. As you can see, it has six seats and it's a sweet ride. Do you have any questions before I lift her up?"

"Yes," Trish blurted out. "Do you have barf bags? What if I get sick up there?"

"Never had that happen," the pilot laughed. "But I guess if it should, I'll have a cleaning job to do when we get back. No bags on board."

As the craft started rising, Riley and Connie looked through the glass at the ground. In the seat behind them, Trish closed her eyes and lowered her head, grabbing hold of whatever her hands could find and squeezing tightly. After a couple of minutes, she began to feel a little more at ease. She even turned to look down before quickly twirling her head back to look straight ahead. By the time they got to the northern side of Adairsville, she was relatively calm and able to focus on the scenery below.

Riley was watching the buildings, houses, and roads, hoping to see a metallic green Kia Soul. *It's amazing how much traffic there is on Highway 140 and how little in other parts of town on a Saturday afternoon.* "Look, there's home right below us," Riley said, indicating the little steeple pointing up at them. As they flew west and then south, Riley gave close attention to the buildings she knew to be vacant but was disappointed not to see anything that looked like a green Kia. Southwest of town, Riley spotted a vehicle traveling ahead of them on a country road. Her first impression was that it could be what she was looking for: a smaller car that appeared to be a light shade of green. As they got closer, she could see it was the wrong shade of green as well as the wrong model.

"I thought you might like to see this," the pilot said as he turned his head in their direction. "That's Barnsley Gardens. Beautiful from up here, isn't it? I have actually flown people in and out of there several times."

Riley marveled at the dark green grass that covered the links. The course seemed to be at capacity; she could not imagine it otherwise on a Saturday afternoon at this time of the year. One of her professors at Emory had been delighted when she arranged for him and three of his friends to play a Saturday round two weeks earlier. It had not been easy to get a tee time at the popular course. Fact is, it would have been impossible had it not been for Amos's connections. Amos seemed to always know someone who could get the job done, regardless of what the job was.

The orderly way in which the resort was arranged was especially impressive from the air. Even the quality of the landscaping was striking from their vantage point. The ruins of the original Italian style mansion stood strong in the midst of it all, looking noble even in its present state. "That's our world-class resort, developed on a pre-Civil War plantation," Riley told Trish, whose color had returned to normal from its earlier pale white.

"In the past, it was known as Woodlands," Connie, the local history buff, explained. "The gardens are exquisite. The original owner was a shipping magnate from Savannah. He and his people brought back rare bushes and plants from all over the world. The owners have done a great job of restoring those gardens. I believe they have even taken them a level beyond the originals."

"We're going to eat at one of the restaurants there sometime next week," Riley announced.

"Wow," Trish responded, looking down to take it all in. Her excitement seemed to help her recover from her earlier fears. "That's beautiful."

From there they flew northeast, all the way out to the Pine Log community. Riley pointed out the historic Pine Log Methodist Church and Campground. Shortly after that, they flew over the cabin that Riley recognized the one-time home of early twentieth century novelist Corra Harris. She and Kirby had visited there the previous summer. After that they saw mostly trees until they were back at the airport and on the ground again. The entire trip had taken just a little more than an hour. Riley said nothing to any of her companions, but she was disappointed she hadn't seen the car she set out to find. But it wasn't wasted time. She and her friends had taken their first helicopter ride. Even Trish had seemingly enjoyed it once her nerves settled down.

They drove back to Adairsville, where they all gathered around the Edwards' big dining table for Carol's vegetable soup and cornbread. After taking a few bites, Trish declared, "You're right, Riley. It's worth the trip here."

"It should be delicious. She's had enough practice," Amos told them. "A person can't get sick in this town without getting some of Carol's soup. She never makes it without preparing some for us as well—not that I'm complaining!" He lowered his voice so only Riley could hear him. "I could eat it every day, and sometimes do."

After dinner, Amos insisted they make homemade ice cream. Trish's viewpoint had always been, why make it at home when you can buy it in a store? After eating a large bowl of Amos and Carol's peach cream, she had her answer. Nothing purchased in a store could match it. It was almost ten o'clock before Riley and Trish settled back into the little nest that Riley called home. They talked for another two hours before turning in. Riley fell asleep quickly but awoke around two o'clock. She tossed and turned for much of the remainder of the night as her mind refused to abandon Kaylene. Somehow, she had to find the Kid. *Time is running out.*

CHAPTER 8

Riley usually rode to Sunday morning church with Amos and Carol. Knowing she and Trish needed to get away as soon as possible to meet Mike and Nathan, she decided to drive her own car on this particular Lord's Day. It took her a good ten minutes to convince Trish it was okay to go to church dressed for the picnic. Trish was accustomed to a formal service that required dressing accordingly. "I've always been taught to dress for church as you would dress to meet the most important person you know. If you had an appointment with the president, wouldn't you dress in your finest?" Trish asked.

Riley thought about that for a moment before responding, "Not necessarily. If he were my father, I'd probably wear something sort of casual. I usually like to wear my best for church too. That was our practice when I was growing up, but I don't think it's necessary. You'll find people in our church dressed to the hilt, and others who come very casually. The Bible doesn't seem to say much about clothing beyond instructing us to dress modestly." Riley wasn't sure Trish was one hundred percent convinced, but nevertheless, she dressed down enough to enjoy a picnic.

They arrived ahead of most of the Sunday school crowd, giving Riley the opportunity to introduce Trish to Pastor Jensen and his wife Jane. Soon, twelve middle school students had gathered, and Riley enthusiastically shared the account of Paul and Silas in prison as recorded in Acts 16. Riley missed Kaylene's comments and questions. She observed that Marcel, Kaylene's customary companion in class, appeared much quieter than usual.

After Sunday school, they moved into the auditorium for the worship service. On the way in, they met police chief Charley Nelson, his wife Tanya, and their little four-month-old, Davis.

"Did you say he is the chief?" Trish asked. "He looks terribly young to be chief."

"As far as I know, he's still the youngest chief of police in the state. I think twenty-seven or twenty-eight years old. But he's a good one, and he loves the people of this town. Did you notice their son's name is Davis? Davis and Deidra Morgan's child is called Charley. As you might guess, the two men are very close. Remind me sometime to tell you about their relationship."

As always, the service moved briskly with no dead time or unnecessary speeches from the platform. The song service, a combination of traditional and contemporary, was energetic. Riley had grown up with the old hymns and appreciated the opportunity to sing a couple of them. She so wanted Trish to like the service. Her glances in her friend's direction told her she had nothing to worry about. She was focused and very much in a worship mode. Riley relaxed and enjoyed the service. Pastor Jensen's message on Barnabas about being an encourager was one of the best she had heard him present. The service was over shortly after twelve o'clock, but their plan for getting out quickly was spoiled by several people who wanted to greet Riley and meet her friend. It was almost twelve-thirty before they were able to drive out of the parking lot. That would enable them to be at their meeting place well before one o'clock.

Mike's car was the only one left in the parking lot of the Calhoun church when they pulled in.

"Please hurry, that fried chicken I prepared has been on my mind for a while," Mike called out.

"You've never fried chicken in your life," Riley retorted, getting into the front seat.

"Check the picnic basket," Mike challenged.

"Look into the picnic basket and see if there is any fried chicken," Riley told Trish, who got into the back seat with Nathan and the big basket.

Trish pushed the red and white cloth that lined the basket aside and peeped, "Looks like chicken to me," she announced.

"Where did you get it?" Riley asked. "KFC?"

"That chicken came straight from a frying pan in the Unger kitchen," Mike assured her.

"Yeah, but which Unger did the frying?" Riley enquired.

"Well, since we are still in a church parking lot, I cannot fib. Grandmother Unger did the actual cooking, but I supervised."

They appreciated the air Mike's car provided as the midday sun beamed brightly. The forty-five-minute drive to the top of Fort Mountain was pleasant, though Riley was a little concerned for Trish when they reached the higher elevations with the valley clearly visible below. "Don't you people do anything on level ground?" she asked, turning her eyes away from the beautiful scenery below. But all was well when they drove into the park entrance and quickly located a picnic table under a large oak tree.

They enjoyed the food along with lively conversation. Afterwards, Mike spread a blanket on the ground and stretched out. Riley continued to sit at the table while Nathan and Trish decided to follow the trail leading up the hill to the tower. They had seen several people move further up the mountain and wanted to see what the attraction was.

Riley studied Mike, lying on his back on the blanket with his eyes closed. *He really is extremely handsome,* she thought, giving attention to his thick dark hair and his thin physique. A year older than her, he was mature for his age. One of his most appealing attributes was his devotion to his Lord and his church. He was kind. She could not remember him ever raising his voice to her. At her urging, they had agreed not to limit their social activity exclusively to one another; however, they still found themselves together frequently. She knew that Mike, for the past few months, had been ready to commit himself to her alone. No doubt, most girls would be flattered and ready to accept the life such a man could offer. *No, it's not him,* she decided. *I don't know a better man. It's just that I'm not ready.*

Riley was suddenly aware that Mike had opened his eyes and was smiling. He caught her looking directly at him. She giggled and he laughed before sitting up. "Was there a fly on my nose?" he asked.

"No, I was just noticing what a handsome man you are. Mike, I hope you know I admire you greatly. You're a good man. Sometimes I think I'm being unfair and maybe a bit unkind toward you. It's just that I don't want to make any commitments until I know I'm ready to do so."

"I understand," Mike replied. "You know where I stand. I would be ready to start our life together tomorrow if you were willing. But since you are reluctant, I'm hanging around until you, hopefully, are ready. And if that never happens, I've given it my best shot."

"Thank you for being so understanding and patient. You're one in a million."

"No, I don't think so. I'm just a man who knows he can't force his will on the woman he loves. And I do love you, Riley."

"I know that and there is no doubt in my mind about my love for you. I just don't know if it is the kind of love that would enable two people to build a life together." Riley had not intended for the conversation to go in this direction. She was relieved when she heard a man's voice.

"Excuse me, could you tell me the way to the tower?" the voice asked.

"Yes sir, I believe it's that way," Mike pointed to the trail Nathan and Trish had taken earlier.

They walked around the immediate area watching the birds and squirrels. "Have you heard anything from your friend Dave about that open spot on the force in Floyd County?" Riley asked.

"I had lunch with him yesterday. He put in a good word for me. He thinks I have a good shot at getting it, but I don't know if I really want to make that change. It would mean considerably more money, but I enjoy being part of the Adairsville force. Chief Nelson is so easy to work with, and he's been so good to me. I've just about talked myself out of it."

"You know how I feel about it. I like having you in Adairsville where I can keep tabs on you," Riley told him with an impish smile on her face. "I love running into you around town and I like the fact that there is less crime than in some other places, and thus a safer environment in which to work."

"If I continue to work in Adairsville, I will probably try to find a part-time second job, or some means of increasing my income. My salary is just not goin' to do it for me down the road."

They stopped to watch two girls who both looked to be around ten years old playing catch with a softball. "Hey, look at the one with the braided hair. She's good. She doesn't throw like a girl at all."

"I'll ignore that remark," Riley grimaced. "Those kids are having a great time," she added as she not only watched the two girls with the ball, but three younger children playing tag.

"Yeah, I love watchin' them. That's one of the bonuses of patrollin' the various neighborhoods in Adairsville. Some days they're everywhere. A few of them have become so accustomed to us that they wave when we pass. I consider protecting those children a big part of my job. Yesterday when I was having lunch with Dave, he told me they received a call Friday evening from someone who reported seein' a child with her hands tied behind her being dragged into a car."

Riley stopped in her tracks. "Was she rescued?" she immediately asked.

"No, not that I've heard. I'm sure it took a little time to get someone to Shannon. By then, there was no trace of a man or a little girl with hands tied."

"Where in Shannon did this happen?" Riley asked.

Mike looked closely at Riley. "Why are you so interested?" he asked.

"I don't know, I guess I'm just concerned for that poor little girl's safety."

Riley's face had suddenly turned a little pale. Mike continued to look at her as he responded, "I think it happened out near the railroad tracks on the road that runs between the park and the old factory building."

That's it! That's where they are. They drove into the old school yard, and not finding it a good place to hide, went a short distance farther to the old mill. Why didn't I check that out when we were over there? I've got to get there as soon as possible. Riley imagined all sorts of horrible things happening to Kaylene. The beautiful day had suddenly turned into a nightmare.

"Mike, could we go home as soon as Nathan and Trish return? I don't feel so well."

"I noticed you were turnin' a little pale. What's wrong?"

"It's no big deal, just one of those things. I'll be alright when I can get home and pull myself together."

Mike knew better than to push a lady about why she felt badly. They sat on a bench, mostly in silence, waiting for Nathan and Trish to return. Mike continued to glance toward Riley from time to time. She desperately wanted to tell him the whole story but knew she would be risking Kaylene's life by doing so. *Where are they? They could have walked to the tower and back three times by now,* she agonized. She tried to talk to Mike to keep him from becoming suspicious, but her mind didn't seem capable of holding any thought beyond her concern for the safety of her little friend.

It was probably fifteen more minutes before the couple returned. Both Nathan and Trish looked surprised when Mike announced that Riley didn't feel well and that they would have to go.

Not wanting to carry on a conversation once they were in the car, Riley laid her head back on the seat's headrest and closed her eyes. She hated deceiving her friends, but what else could she do? "I'll drive you home and Nathan can follow us in your car," Mike suggested when they reached the church parking lot where she had left her car.

"That's kind of you, but I can handle it, and if I find I can't, Trish can drive," she told him, getting under the wheel of her vehicle.

Trish was obviously puzzled when after a few blocks they turned south on Highway 53 rather than heading toward Adairsville. "No, I'm not lost," Riley said. "We've got to get to Shannon as soon as possible."

"My guess is that it would be useless to ask you why," Trish said, continuing to stare at her friend. "If I'm right, while we were on that mountain, Mike unknowingly told you something related to this mission we seem to be on. Whatever he told you is the motivation for this trip to Shannon. Shame on you, girl. You scared us all half to death, and you're not sick at all."

"I'm sorry I worried you. The truth is that I am sick, but not in the way you thought. Please trust me," she pleaded as she stepped on the accelerator to push their speed to the legal limit. "We've got to get there with enough time left before dark to search that old building."

Trish thought it best not to inquire about the identity of the building.

When they crossed the railroad to enter the village, Riley pointed to the left. "That's the place we've got to search," she announced.

"That building is huge!" Trish said, examining the abandoned mill. "There must be hundreds of places to hide in there."

"As I understand it, there's not near as much building as there once was. The older part of the structure was demolished several years ago. The first step we need to take is to drive along both the east and west sides of the building. Then we need to take a look at the back. We are on the lookout for any car that might be near or inside the fence, but especially a metallic green Kia Soul."

"Oh, yes," Trish responded. "The infamous green Kia." Cruising the premises, they saw no vehicle inside the fence or parked anywhere near it.

"Our next move is to find a place to park, so we can locate a way inside the fence to search the building," Riley declared.

"You've got to be kidding. You want to go inside that place?" Trish protested.

"I don't really want to, but I have no choice," Riley declared. "You don't have to go. You can remain with the car if you wish."

"No way, lady. I'm going where you go. It's one for all, and all for one. I'll be about three steps behind you."

Riley parked the car in front of the old company store, now vacant. They marched along the east side of the complex to the fence where

Riley took a long look in all directions to make sure they would not be seen. Then she led the way along the fence line, hoping for a gate or opening that would allow them to enter. Obviously, the fence wasn't being well maintained. It was leaning in places, and they saw several small breaks. After about five minutes they came to a place where a section of the fence was damaged enough for the two of them to crawl through. Now the trick was to find a way to get inside the building. Riley headed for the back of the building where she had seen several doors when they were surveying the old structure. She pushed on three different doors before she found one that would open. Trish had dropped back a little more than her customary three steps. "Do you have your phone?" Riley asked in almost a whisper. "There are no windows to give light to this part of the building. We'll only use our lights when we must. And we have to be very quiet."

"Don't you worry about that. I'll be quieter than a sleeping mouse," Trish nervously declared.

Even in the dimness of the windowless building, the now empty space looked massive. They walked for maybe ten minutes, with Riley occasionally using the light of her phone to examine their immediate surroundings. "Let's completely stop for a couple of minutes and listen closely for any noises," she suggested. They stood perfectly still but heard nothing. "Come on," Riley said quietly. "Let's take that corridor to the left."

"Are you sure you want to take any detours? We could get lost in here, you know."

"Don't worry. Just stay close to me. We're not going to get lost."

Shortly after taking the turn, Riley thought she heard a noise. She abruptly stopped, raising her arm as a signal for her companion to do likewise. In the darkness Trish didn't see the gesture and bumped squarely into Riley's back, knocking her forward a couple of feet. "Are you okay?" Riley asked.

"Everything but my nose. I think I broke it on your backbone. It would be good if you could let me know when you are coming to a stop, since your break lights don't seem to be working."

Recouping, they moved ahead, stepping lightly. Again, Riley thought she heard a noise. It seemed to come from behind them. "Listen," she said. "Did you hear that?"

"I heard it. It sounded like someone bumping into something," Trish replied with a shaky voice.

They froze and listened carefully, but the noise had subsided. Then it happened. Out of the darkness, they heard the roar of a man's voice. "I've got a gun pointed in your direction, and I assure you, I know how to use it!"

CHAPTER 9

Suddenly there was light on the two startled young ladies. "Who are you?" the man's voice demanded.

"I'm Riley Gordan, and this is my friend Trish." Riley's voice reflected her panic.

"I guess you are. I thought you looked familiar." The light moved toward them. "What're you doin' here? You know you could've been killed."

With her initial panic now tapering off, Riley recognized the voice. "I suspect we're here for the same reason as you. We're looking for Kaylene."

Nate Bannister approached them, a pistol in his right hand. With his arm hanging at his side, the gun was pointed at the floor. There was a large flashlight in his left hand. "Stan told me Wilma confided in you."

"She didn't exactly confide. I sort of drew it out of her at a time when she was too emotionally distraught to resist. I guess you heard, as we did, that a young girl about Kaylene's age was dragged into a car near here Friday evening?"

"I have a number of friends in law enforcement. Sometimes it's not hard to get them to talkin'," the older gentleman told them. "You know you're puttin' yourself in grave danger by bein' here, don't you? These people, whoever they are, are not playin' games."

Trish stood silently with her mouth open before eventually finding a seat on a small piece of abandoned equipment that had been pushed against the wall. When Nate looked in her direction, she said, "Excuse me, sir, but I've got to sit down."

"We're being extremely careful," Riley insisted.

"A moment ago, you weren't careful enough to avoid gettin' blown away if I had been one of the kidnappers," Nate pointed out to her. "You just need to stay out of the way and let me handle this. Now, go on home and forget you saw me here."

"We're on our way, but please, for my peace of mind, could you tell me if you've found anything?"

"There's no one here now but us. I've been searching for more than three hours and found nothin' but some trash. Someone may have been hidin' here recently, but if they were, they have gone. Now, missy, I want you gone, and I want you to stay out of this. I can't be worryin' about anyone else's safety."

"Yes sir, Mr. Bannister. Trish, let's get out of this gentleman's way." Riley turned and started walking back in the direction from which they came. Trish jumped up from her perch to follow closely, occasionally glancing back in Bannister's direction, obviously making sure the gun was still pointed at the floor.

"So that's the famous Nate Bannister," Trish commented when she figured they were beyond his hearing distance. "Cantankerous old coot, isn't he? Speaks loudly and carries a big gun."

"He's a nice man," Riley assured her. "You would see a completely different person under other circumstances."

"Where do you suppose his car is parked? We didn't see any other cars in the vicinity. He's a little long-in-the-tooth to have walked the ten or twelve miles from Adairsville, don't you think?"

"I don't know. You've got to remember, he was a professional athlete," Riley reminded her.

"A hundred years ago!" Trish sarcastically responded.

"I suspect he parked in the lot over at the park," Riley told her. "Come on. Let's hurry to the car."

***

"I can't believe what I'm payin' for this hole-in-the-wall motel," Houston complained. "It's eatin' up our profits, you know, and it's all because of you," he added, looking sternly at the woman, whose face was bruised. "We could still be usin' that old mill building if you had done your job and kept the girl inside. I can't trust you to handle anything. If it's goin' to get done, I have to do it."

"You've already made that clear," the woman said quietly, rubbing the bruise on her face. "At least we have beds to sleep on and a TV to watch here."

"One more day and it'll be over. Tomorrow is when the old man will announce he's steppin' aside," Houston reminded her. "We can collect our money and head home."

The woman looked at the girl. She appeared to be asleep, lying face down on one of the beds with her hands tied behind her. "What will we do with her?" she asked in a whisper.

"You know what we have to do. We can't leave her walkin' around to later identify us and maybe send us to prison for life."

"Houston, you can't do that! She's just a kid. Her life is just getting started."

"You're wrong about that. It's about to end. Just as soon as we hear the old man has pulled out of the election, it's bye, bye, birdie. Her age makes no difference. Twelve or twenty, to leave her around would spell real trouble for us. We've got to get rid of her."

"Why can't we take her a couple of hours down the road and release her in the woods? We would be long gone by the time she's rescued."

"Think, woman. Think about everything she's overheard us say over the last few days. Don't you know she has learned enough about us that the law would be waitin' for us when we got home? No! She has to die, or we'll likely spend the rest of our lives in prison. And notice I said *we*. You are just as guilty as me. If we are caught, both of us will pay the consequences. Fact is, I think when the time comes, I'll let you pull the trigger. Yeah, that's what I'm goin' to do. That's how you can make up for all your blunders. You'll be the trigger person."

The woman hung her head and rubbed the bruised spot on her face but said nothing more.

Kaylene lay on her stomach, her face pressed into the pillow, but her eyes were wide open and her ears attentive. She knew she had one more day to find a crack to squeeze through, or it would all be over for her. *Lord, you know I don't ask you for much, but today I really need you. If you don't help me, I'm never goin' to see Mom and Dad again. Nate is goin' to be so lonely, and I guess I'll never get to nursin' school. Please help me! Show me a way out of this mess. I know you can do it.*

***

On Monday morning Riley woke before daylight. *One more day. If we don't find her before tomorrow morning, Nate will withdraw and whoever is holding Kaylene may decide they don't need her any longer, and maybe can't afford to let her live for fear she would identify them.* She couldn't remember ever feeling more frustrated. There had to be something she could do, but what? Should she go to Amos, Mike, or Chief Nelson? Wilma would get over her breaking her word if it led to Kaylene's rescue, but what if it didn't? What if it resulted in her death? No! She couldn't play Russian roulette with Kaylene's life. She had no idea about where to search next. Obviously, they had narrowly missed the kidnappers and their victim a couple of times, but there were no more clues. Riley remembered something she heard her dad say in a sermon back in her high school days. He commented that he had often heard exasperated people say they had tried everything else, and now, as a last resort, they would pray. "They should have tried prayer first, not as a last resort. We get the process upside down," he remarked.

Maybe that's my problem. I've been trying to do it myself. Riley spent the next fifteen minutes on her back in her bed asking for the help of the person she knew she should have seriously consulted earlier. Then she got out of bed to go into the kitchen for coffee. She still didn't know what to do next, but the hopelessness was gone. It was in his hands now.

She was surprised when Trish joined her in the kitchen a few minutes later. This was the earliest she had gotten up since arriving. When they were seated at the table with their coffee, Trish remarked, "I didn't sleep much last night. I used a lot of the time I was awake praying for your little girl."

Riley felt certain today was going to be eventful. She had no idea what it would entail, but it would be a momentous day.

***

"I'm worried about Riley," Amos told Carol before picking up his coffee cup. "She's not herself. Something is weighing heavy on her mind."

"Do you have any idea what it is?" his wife asked him.

"She all but admitted to me that there's a problem but indicated telling me would compromise her integrity. I wouldn't want her to do that, so I haven't pushed her."

"I wish Kirby were here. Maybe she would confide in him," Carol remarked. Feeling Max's head rubbing against her ankle, she got up and went to the cabinet, where she took out the cat food box. She poured some of the contents into Max's bowl before returning to her place at the table.

"Well, he's not here, but we don't have to know the details of her uneasiness to help. We can pray about it. God knows exactly what's on her heart," Amos reminded his wife.

"Then we best do that," Carol suggested, reaching out to take her husband's hand.

Amos didn't hesitate. In moments he was asking the Lord to intervene on Riley's behalf, to help her with whatever she was wrestling with. Carol offered a prayer of her own after her husband had concluded his.

Amos's phone started ringing before his wife had finished. He answered immediately after hearing Carol say "Amen."

"Hello? Yes, Marvin, we are looking for a car like that . . ."

***

The girls were already dressed for the day when Amos rang Riley's doorbell a few minutes before nine o'clock. "I thought you would want to know that I received a call from my friend, Marvin, about seeing a metallic green Kia Soul. He saw it in the Motel 6 parking lot in Calhoun while they were picking up the garbage this morning. He said it had a Bibb County license plate. Do you think that could be the one you are searching for?"

"Motel 6 is on Highway 53 near the I-75 exit ramp, isn't it?" Riley asked.

"Yes, that's the one," Amos said.

"Thank you, Amos," she said, hugging his neck. "You are amazing. Please pray that this is the one."

"Would you like for me to go with you to check it out?" Amos asked.

Riley thought about that for a moment before answering. "No, but thank you for offering. Trish and I will take a look, and if we need you, we'll give you a call."

"You be sure to do that," he told her. "I'll be around here and available all day if you need me. Bill and the Cleaning Crew are just a telephone call away, and you know how much they love doing things for you. Plenty of help if you need it."

Amos continued to stand at the door as if he didn't want to leave. "Thank you, Amos," Riley said. "That's one of the reasons I like being in Adairsville. There's always someone offering to help."

Amos smiled and reluctantly turned to walk back down the hallway to his living quarters. He stopped and looked back in Riley's direction, but then slowly continued his stroll back to his own place.

"I guess we're going to take another trip to Calhoun," Riley told Trish. Minutes later, they were in Riley's car and driving north on Interstate 75 at seventy miles per hour. *This could be it*, Riley reasoned. *They wouldn't want to bring her to an Adairsville motel. It would be too easy for her to be recognized there. It is a straight shot up Highway 53 from Shannon to the Calhoun Motel 6. If they left the old mill, a motel would be the logical place to go. But how can I get into the room to check it out?*

Riley was pondering possible strategies when Trish asked, "Do you think this could pan out, or is it just another wild goose chase?"

"Maybe it's just wishful thinking on my part, but I've got a strong feeling that we are on the right path. We'll know shortly. That's our exit just ahead." Riley turned onto Highway 53 and an instant later into the motel parking lot. There were several cars still in the lot, and one of them was, indeed, a metallic green Kia Soul. She pulled into a space behind the elusive vehicle.

"What are we going to do now? Even if that is the car, how will we know who is driving it?" Trish asked.

"I've got an idea," Riley replied.

"I thought you might."

"Get out of the car as quietly as possible and follow me." Trish followed her instructions. "Now stand to my left." When Trish was in place, Riley braced herself by putting her left hand on Trish's shoulder. Then she raised her right leg and with the bottom of her shoe pounded the Kia's passenger side taillight. The first blow failed to do the job, so she repeated the process, this time kicking a little harder. Now there was a six-inch break on the taillight cover. "That should do it," she whispered.

"Why did you do that? What if this isn't the car we have been searching for?" Trish asked in a bit of a panic.

"In that case, I will pay for a new taillight cover," Riley told her. "Now I want you to go over there." Riley pointed to the area where there was a stairway leading to the second floor. "Stay out of sight and keep your phone in your hand. If I raise my left hand above my head, call 911 immediately. Tell them a little girl has been kidnapped, and they need to get here as quickly as possible."

"What are you going to do?" Trish asked with the note of panic still in her voice.

"I don't have time to explain now. Go on over there and stay out of sight. Do you remember what you are to do when I raise my left hand above my head?"

"When you raise your left hand, not your right, but your left, I am to call 911 and tell the authorities they are to get here immediately because a little girl has been kidnapped."

"Perfect," Riley told her. "Now go."

When Trish was in place, Riley nervously walked to the door of the motel room closest to the green Kia. She knocked loudly. A middle-aged lady dressed in jeans and a sweatshirt opened the door. "Hi," Riley said with a smile as big as she could muster. "I was wondering if that green Kia is yours?" She pointed in the direction of the car in question.

"No. That's my car over there," the woman told her, pointing toward another of the parked cars. I think the one you are asking about belongs to the people in the room next door," she said. "But if I were you, honey, I would think twice before going over there," she added.

"Why do you say that?" Riley asked.

"The guy I saw looked like a pretty rough character and some of the language I've heard coming from there was pretty bad."

"Thanks for the warning," Riley said. "I'll be cautious."

Riley wasn't anxious to go to the door that had been pointed out to her, but she knew she had to. Before knocking, she looked to see if Trish was still in place. She was there, peeping around the corner. Riley knocked. The door opened. Standing before her was a man who appeared as if he hadn't shaved in several days. His shirt was open, and his feet were bare. He obviously had not yet combed his hair. He opened the door just enough to slide outside, then closed the door behind him. Riley was disappointed she couldn't get a look inside the room.

"Can I do something for you, sweety?" he asked with a twisted smile that made Riley extremely uncomfortable.

"Yes sir, is that your green car over there?" she asked purposely speaking loud enough for anyone on the inside to hear her voice. She pointed in the direction of the green Kia.

"Why do you want to know?" he asked with a suspicious look.

"Well, I'm really sorry, but I bumped into your car and broke your taillight," she told him.

"You mean to say that with only a few cars scattered on this lot, you hit my car?" The man started a blue streak of profanities.

"There's hardly any damage. I'll pay you for repairs. Let me show you." She started walking toward the car. The man mumbled as he followed along behind her on bare feet.

***

Inside the motel room, the Kid lifted her head when she heard the voice outside. She knew that voice. She had listened to it in Sunday school every Sunday for the past few weeks. She jumped to her feet and looked toward the woman. "You'll have to kill me or at least wrestle me to the floor to keep me from goin' through that door," she said, as she started slowly moving in that direction.

The woman smiled, opened the door, and said, "Run child. Run as fast as those little legs will carry you."

"Miss Riley, I'm here, I'm here!" Kaylene cried as she ran through the open door with her hands tied behind her.

CHAPTER 10

Riley heard Kaylene's cry and turned to see her running toward her. "No. Go that way," she shouted, motioning toward Trish, who stepped out of the shadows to hold her arms out to the girl.

Seeing Houston near Riley, Kaylene grasped the danger and redirected her flight toward Trish. Riley raised her left arm and yelled to Trish, "Call now." She saw Trish putting the phone to her ear.

Houston glanced toward Riley, then back at Kaylene, then immediately started sprinting in the girl's direction. His scheme was over if she made good her escape. Riley had no time to ponder her next move. She took off behind the barefoot man, using every ounce of energy she had. It took her about thirty feet to get almost close enough to reach out and touch his back. She dove at the lower part of his body with both hands extended, but only managed to latch her right hand onto one of his ankles. It was enough. He went sliding on his stomach across the asphalt. When he stopped skidding, he turned over on his back, shook his head side to side, and then sat up before getting to his feet. Seeing Riley still on the ground, he took several steps toward her with curses spewing out of his mouth. He kicked at her head with his right foot. She moved quickly to the left, managing to narrowly evade his vicious attack.

But the man wasn't through yet. He reached under the back of his shirttail and pulled a pistol from beneath his belt. With an evil grimace on his face, he pointed it at Riley. *I guess this is it*, she thought, unable to move. *He can't miss from that distance.*

She heard Kaylene cry out from Trish's arms, "No! Don't you dare harm Miss Riley!" Houston turned his head in the direction of the cry. He saw that several other people had come out of their rooms and were now witnessing his every action. There was a moment of silent indecision. "Your time will come," he muttered before he started running toward his car, calling for the woman to follow him. She entered the passenger side at about the same time as he opened the other door. They were out of the parking lot, tires squealing, in an instant. Riley rose just in time to watch as the metallic green Kia speeded toward Interstate 75. She had barely gotten to her feet when Kaylene, with her hands now free, ran into her arms.

"Are you alright?" Trish asked Riley, observing small cuts and scratches on her arms and tears in her clothes.

"I'm wonderful," she declared. "And what about you Kaylene? How are you?"

"Me too, I'm wonderful too," she replied, hugging Riley's neck with most of her strength.

The Calhoun police were there in full force within five minutes. "Looks like you got the job done," Riley smiled at Trish.

"I think we both did our job," Trish told her. "Looks like Frankenstein and his bride got away, but the Kid is safe, and that's what matters. You are one awesome chick," she added.

"You're alright yourself. We've always been a pretty good team," Riley said as she reached over to pull her close to her side. "Now, I've got to make a call that is going to make two parents and an older gentleman very happy."

That happiness was evident forty minutes later when the trio was reunited with their missing Kid at Calhoun police headquarters. There was a stop at the hospital emergency unit for the sakes of both Riley and Kaylene, then there were a lot of questions by the authorities for each of them. It was late afternoon before they were back in Adairsville. Riley ached all over, but she decided she had never been happier.

***

The two days following Kaylene's rescue were busy but delightful days. There were visits from the GBI, Bartow County sheriff, and even

Chief Charley Nelson of the Adairsville department. "I don't have jurisdiction in the matter since the kidnapping took place outside the city limits, and your escapade was in Gordon County," Charley told her. "But I like to stay abreast of what's going on." They talked for half an hour. Riley tried hard to provide answers to Charley's questions.

"How's little Davis?" Riley asked as the chief was exiting.

"He's great," Charley instantly answered. "Growing like a weed, and like his namesake, getting spunkier every day."

On Tuesday afternoon, Riley received a visit from newspaper reporter Susan Peak, whom she had met at Kaylene's interview. "I tried to get an interview with Kaylene and her parents, but they're shying away from media activity," she explained. "I guess I'll have to get my story from you." Riley answered her questions as best she could while trying to stay clear of revealing information for which the authorities would be the best source. Susan told her before leaving that she should plan to get Wednesday's paper. "They're holding the presses for this story," the reporter announced.

Riley and Trish met Mike and Nathan for breakfast at the Little Rock Café on Wednesday morning before Mike went on duty. As usual, the little building was packed and buzzing with Adairsville citizens craving the good food and special camaraderie the establishment provided each morning. "Why did we come here rather than the Cracker Barrel?" Trish asked.

"Cracker Barrel is great, but you can't get what's here at Cracker Barrel," Riley responded. "The food here is certainly worth the trip, but the neat thing about this place is that it is where the personalities that make up the heartbeat of our little town gather. Monday through Friday mornings they meet here to tell their tales. See that group over there?" She nodded toward a large round table in a corner where eight men, in dress ranging from suit and tie to the uniform of a mechanic, were carrying on a lively conversation. "The big guy facing us is Dean Nelson. They tell me he may be the best football player to come out of Adairsville High—could probably have played professionally, but he left the university before the end of his freshman year to come home and marry his sweetheart. He's the older brother of our police chief and a wizard of a mechanic. He's also a real sweetheart.

"The man in the tie and jacket is Al Jensen, the president of our largest bank," Riley continued. "Very little business gets done in this town without going through him. The gentleman beside him with the red hair is Red Edwards, owner of the Adairsville hardware store, which Uncle James tried unsuccessfully for years to acquire. I don't know his given name, and I don't know if anyone else does. He's just Red to everyone. The man to his left is beloved fire chief Brad Dewelt. And you've met Davis Morgan, bookseller, preacher, police chaplain, and the town's master sleuth. He's put more than one bad guy behind bars. One of them did put him on those crutches, though.

"There's Mayor Ellison and high-roller Kenneth Cotes, over there," Mike motioned with his head. "And isn't that the representative from the Outdoor Sportsman with them?"

"Yes, I think you're right. That's Jason Purcell. He showed up at Amos and Carol's dinner the other night," Riley agreed.

"No doubt, a lot of big business being transacted at that table," Mike laughed.

"At least in their imaginations," Riley grinned. She thought she knew the name when Mike mentioned Kenneth Cotes, but at first it didn't click. Then it came to her. That was the man who thought Nate shot his dog—the contractor. She looked closely at him. She had been working hard to refrain from judging people by their appearance but found herself unsuccessful with this man. His dark, slicked back hair and beady, close-set eyes said scoundrel to her. She was immediately ashamed of herself for reaching such a conclusion based on nothing more than a glance and a brief helping of hearsay. *He may be a wonderful person*, she told herself before looking up to see a waitress standing beside their table.

"Good morning, folks. May I take your order?" the waitress asked while pouring their coffee. "Looks like you have some new friends with you today."

"This is Trish, a special friend from my college days, and Nathan, a youth pastor in Calhoun who is new to our area. Guys, this is Brenda, the best waitress in this town," she told them.

After Brenda chatted for a moment and then took their order, she left to deliver it to the kitchen. "Brenda's a wonderful mother of two bright children and sings like an angel. Everyone adores her," Riley said.

"Seems like you know everyone in town," Trish remarked. "How did you accomplish that by being here just on weekends?"

"Well, don't forget that I was here all of last summer. It's a small town and people, for the most part, are amicable, making it easy to get to know them. A couple of years ago, I would never have dreamed I could become so attached to a small town."

"And what about you, Mike? Do you feel the same way about Adairsville?" Trish asked.

"I've lived ten miles away in Calhoun all my life, but I do enjoy my work here. Just wish they would pay more."

"I know you were on duty the last couple of days. How has it gone?" Nathan asked Mike.

"It hasn't been nearly as exciting as Riley and Trish's Monday adventure," Mike responded. "I've written several traffic tickets and picked up Ole Buster yesterday. That's about all the business I've done."

"Who's Ole Buster?" Trish asked. "Sounds like a story there."

"Yeah, I'd like to know too. I don't think I've met him yet," Riley broke in.

"I suspect you've seen him staggering down one of our streets at one time or another," Mike responded.

"You mean the old guy with the gray beard and John Deere cap that is always gawking at the ground?" Riley asked.

"Yeah, He's always gawking at the ground when he's not lying on it. From time to time, we take him in and let him spend the night in our holding cell. We sober him up, but two hours after being released, he's smashed again. None of us can figure out where he gets the money for the booze."

"Maybe he's independently wealthy," Trish suggested. "We had an old drunk back home who was loaded in more ways than one."

"No, not Buster. Just about everyone around here knows his story." At that moment the waitress returned with a large tray that held their breakfast. After she placed everyone's food in its proper place, Mike suggested to Nathan that he give thanks for the meal. As they joined hands and bowed their heads, Trish coyly looked around at the people sitting nearby. Nathan offered his brief prayer.

"Now you can continue Mike," Riley begged after the prayer, "I want to hear Buster's story."

"I noticed earlier you called him 'that old man,'" Mike said as he put butter on his toast. "And I know he looks seventy or more, but I'm certain he's not a day over forty-five. He grew up in the Stoners community a couple of miles south of town. The family never had much but were known as good, hard-working people. Buster managed to get through high school even though, as I understand it, he worked second shift in a Calhoun textile mill most of his senior year. A couple of years out of high school, he married Lois, his longtime sweetheart. A year later, they had their first child; I believe it was a boy. Then two girls came along." Mike paused to take a sip of his coffee, then continued. "Buster was promoted to supervisor at the textile mill, and they bought a little house with several acres of ground down in the area where he grew up. I think he was planning to eventually run a few head of cattle on the side. It looked like life was on track for the little family. Then it happened!

"Late one afternoon, Lois was driving home from Cartersville where she had taken the baby to the doctor. The other two children were with her. With a sick infant, she probably hadn't gotten much sleep the previous night and most likely fell asleep. She ran off old Highway 41 coming down Cassville Mountain. She wasn't more than two or three miles from home. All four of them were killed. The baby lingered in a hospital for almost a week before dying. The other three died instantly. They say Buster got drunk the day the baby died and has been plastered every day since. That was over ten years ago. Of course, he lost his job, his house, and all his dignity. We on the force just kinda watch after him. I don't know when he eats except when we bring him in. We try to make sure he gets a square meal or two. After he's gone, it takes us two days to eliminate the odor he brings with him. We don't give him money; if we do, it will go for liquor."

"That's such a sad story," Trish looked and sounded as if she was about to cry.

"My heart aches for people like that," Riley lamented.

"Isn't there a hospital or institution of some kind where he can be helped?" Nathan asked.

"People have tried to get him help, but he'll have none of it. He doesn't want to be helped. He's just going to continue to drink until someday we find him dead in a ditch," Mike declared.

"I want to introduce you to a couple of people, little lady," the voice coming from behind Riley was louder than any other in the room. She knew it had to be Mayor Ellison. Every time she was in his presence, she was tempted to pass on the instructions her mother had often given her: "Use your inside voice."

"This here is Kenneth Cotes, and behind him, Jason Purcell. I think they would like to be business partners with you," he told Riley.

"And this is my good friend from college, Trish Banks and Nathan Bailey, a youth pastor from one of our sister churches in Calhoun. You, of course, know Mike Unger." The mayor glanced at Trish and Nathan and then ignored them.

"Oh yeah, I know Mike. He's one of our finest."

"Mr. Purcell and I got acquainted recently," Riley stated, turning to Purcell. "Kirby should be home in a week or so. He's trying to wind things up in Florida. Give us a call after then."

"Both of these men are good men," the mayor told her. "They can do a lot for our town. Hope you will listen closely to what they tell you. They can be good for you, and for your brother as well."

The two groups chatted for a couple of minutes. "I'm going to have to go to the gym and work off a few of these calories," Jason Purcell told them after commenting on the country breakfast he had just eaten.

"I'm going to work mine off while making a dollar or two," Cotes declared.

After the mayor's party left, the four friends continued to chat. Riley apologized for deceiving them on Sunday and tried to explain her reasoning without attempting to justify it.

"Just remember that I will always be your, uh . . . friend first and a policeman second. You can tell me anything that's on your mind, and I will use that information only as you wish," Mike told her.

"I appreciate that, but I never want to put you on the spot," she declared. "I respect what you do, and I don't want you to ever have to compromise your obligations. I wanted to tell you the whole story, and maybe I should've, but I also had made a promise to the Boyntons, though maybe ill advised. Whether I handled it right, I'm not sure, but I'm elated it turned out well."

"This time it did, but if I ever hear of you putting yourself in that kind of danger again, you're going to have to contend with me," Mike declared.

After a few more minutes of conversation and finishing up their meals, Mike announced that he had to be at work in ten minutes.

"You can stay five more minutes," Riley laughed. "You've only got to walk across the road to report."

When they were outside, Mike turned to Riley and said, "Incidentally, I learned something late yesterday that might interest you. Two men fishing found the body of a woman down in the Altoona area. She seems to fit the description of the woman who kidnapped the Kid. The GBI will compare fingerprints with some found on objects left in the motel room. I'll let you know what I find out."

The color suddenly went out of Riley's face. "Oh no, Mike. That breaks my heart. If she's dead, it's probably because she helped Kaylene escape. Have you heard how the woman died?"

"It's my understanding she appeared to have been brutally beaten to death."

Tears came to Riley's eyes as she dropped her head. "It'll be alright," Mike told her leaning over to embrace her and kiss her on the forehead. "Maybe we'll find out it wasn't her after all."

Mike's news pretty much took the wind out of Riley's sails. The elation she had felt over a bad situation that turned out well was gone. A woman who played a big part in getting Kaylene home was dead. Maybe it was her scheme that killed her.

CHAPTER 11

With Mike and Nathan departing after breakfast to go to their respective jobs, Riley and Trish set out for Kennesaw to do some shopping. They were at the large mall for better than three hours. Trish purchased jeans and a purse. Riley came away with a new pair of shoes and an assortment of clothes and accessories for Judy, Alice, and Louise, the wives of the Cleaning Crew. She would have to make a trip to the outlet mall in Calhoun to buy outfits and surprises for their children, she decided.

"I can't believe you only bought shoes for yourself," Trish remarked. "If I had your resources, I would have to hire someone to help me carry my purchases to the car."

"All through high school and college, I dreamed of the day I could go to the mall and buy whatever I wanted without considering the cost. Now that I have that luxury, I seldom see anything I want, except shoes. All I have to do is walk past a shoe store and suddenly I need shoes," Riley laughed.

"I hope I don't sound sanctimonious, but one of the delights of having financial flexibility has been experiencing the joy that comes with helping those who have needs. I was taught from childhood to extend a helping hand, but I never, until now, understood the deep satisfaction that comes with doing that," she explained. "I'm learning how gratifying it is to reach out to people struggling just to exist—to help give them a little hope. Both Kirby and I feel strongly about that. We don't want to squander what Uncle James left us. We have an obligation to use it well, to benefit as many people as possible. It's a responsibility we don't take lightly. I guess it would be easy for us to give lump sums of money to benevolent organizations, but that's not what we want to do. Many of them are great ministries, but we want to handpick our own projects and be more hands-on with people. Maybe that's selfish. I don't know," Riley said while stopping for a red light.

"I don't think it's selfish. Aren't we supposed to be involved with those who need us? I've always thought there is so much more to philanthropy than writing a check. Sounds to me like you two are on the right track," Trish said.

"I hope so. Sometimes having all this wealth makes me feel a little guilty. We didn't work for it. It was given to us. We don't have it because we deserve it. It's ours because of a generous uncle. Somehow, it just doesn't seem fair."

"I don't want you to feel guilty. So, if you want to unload some of the burden, then as your friend, I'm willing to sacrifice and take some of it off your hands," Trish offered with a giggle.

"Oh, Trish. You'll never change."

"Aren't you glad? You wouldn't love me half as much if I were anything other than that poor confused and awkward girl you first met in Dr. Peterson's grammar class."

They had not been home more than five minutes when the doorbell rang. Both Amos and Carol were at the door. "Come on in and see my new shoes," Riley invited.

Carol held a newspaper in her hand. "We picked up a paper and thought you might like to see it," she explained.

"Oh, yes. I had forgotten that today is the day for Susan's article. Well, let's see what she had to say," Riley said.

Carol handed her the paper, which Riley immediately unfolded. At the top of the front page in bold print were the words, "LOCAL SUNDAY SCHOOL TEACHER RESCUES KIDNAPPED STUDENT." Riley began to silently read the account that dominated the front page. After a minute or two she mumbled, "Oh, no. This makes me sound like some kind of glory-seeking amateur superhero. It reads like a bad movie script. Kaylene was the heroine, not me. People are going to laugh when they see this. I'll never live it down."

"It's not so bad," Amos said. "She got the basic facts right. And people who are acquainted with you know what kind of person you are."

"Kirby has reminded me several times to beware of newspaper reporters. I need to start listening more to my brother," Riley told them.

"Well, I, for one, think it's rather good," Carol declared. "You probably saved that sweet little girl's life. You were clever and brave, and people need to know about it."

"And just think, this could lead to your own comic book series. Right up there with Wonder Woman," Trish teased.

Riley turned to give her a hard stare.

"Oh, come on girl. Don't take life so seriously. Enjoy the good and forget the bad," Trish told her. "Who else is getting this kind of publicity?"

"I wish someone other than me," Riley stammered.

By the time Amos and Carol left, Riley was feeling better about the article but was definitely ready to move on to another topic of conversation. "You've now had opportunities to be with Nathan on three occasions. What do you think?" she asked Trish. "Any chance of you two hitting it off?"

"Umm . . ." Trish appeared to be in deep contemplation for a minute or two. "Let's just say I'm hopeful. I like what I've seen so far, but most of our time together has been with a group. It's hard to really get to know someone like that."

"It was just the two of you strolling along that trail on the mountain last Sunday afternoon. If I remember correctly, you spent a heap of time together getting up and down that short footpath."

"That's true, but that was just a short hike with people coming and going all around us. You get to know a person better by enjoying a candlelight dinner together, or holding hands in the theater, or maybe experiencing a good concert as a couple."

"So, you're interested in the more romantic stuff. I suspect we can arrange for you and Nathan to spend some quality time together. I'll see what I can do."

"I appreciate that, but whatever you do, don't push him. If he's interested in me, that's wonderful. But please don't think you have to provide an escort for me. I'm perfectly happy solo if that's how it turns out. I didn't come down here to find a man."

***

I should be approaching the Georgia–Florida state line any time now, Kirby estimated, driving north along Interstate 75. When he received Amos's call and learned what Riley had been up to, he couldn't remain in St. Pete any longer. He talked with his chief, who agreed that he needed to wrap up his time there a few days early and head for home. Amos's information led him to believe the matter was closed with the rescue of the girl, but who knew? The kidnappers were still at large. In his brief career as a detective, he had learned how vindictive the really bad ones could sometimes be. He had known them to defy all logic to get even with someone who spoiled their schemes; it couldn't hurt for him to be on hand. *And, besides, I can hardly wait to see Connie.* He set his cruise control to a couple miles per hour faster. *They're going to be surprised when I show up for dinner tonight.*

He saw the sign announcing a Waffle House up ahead and decided a cup of coffee would be good. He found a seat immediately upon entering the restaurant. From across the counter, an attractive brunette approached him with a smile, asking, "Can I take your order?"

"Just coffee."

"You sure you don't want a burger and fries with that?"

"Just coffee," he repeated.

The brunette turned around and took a few steps to the right to retrieve a cup and pour Kirby's coffee. She then returned and presented him with his order. "Where you headed?" she asked.

"I'm on my way home to Adairsville, Georgia."

"I'd never heard of Adairsville until this morning," she said.

"Did you have another customer from there?"

"No, I heard it mentioned on TV. In fact, it was on one of the national news programs. It seems that a Sunday school teacher there risked her life to rescue a child from a kidnapper. I believe she actually tackled the man to allow the child to get away. Have you heard about that?"

"Yeah, I got the news yesterday."

"I know it's a small town. Any chance you know the teacher?" she asked.

"Yes, I know her well," Kirby replied.

"Really? She must be one tough cookie."

"She's a princess," he told the waitress.

***

This will be a good place to leave it, Houston decided as he backed the little Kia into the parallel parking spot. It was the only open space he could find in downtown Marietta. *Too hot to drive anymore. I'll be long gone before they figure out this heap was taken in Macon three weeks ago.* He got out of the car and looked around, hoping no one was paying attention to him. Walking briskly down the sidewalk, he left the square and made his way down Church Street, looking for a parking lot with plenty of customers, but no attendant.

He found what he was searching for near the Presbyterian church. He strolled to the middle of the lot, trying not to attract attention. He knew the full key ring of auto jigglers in his pocket would enable him to get into most cars. The screwdriver he carried would make it possible to start the ignition. He would pick out a good car, one that wouldn't draw a lot of attention. Almost all of them were better than what he was accustomed to. *These Marietta people have good taste in automobiles.* A late model white Ford Taurus got his attention. *It's nice and clean, and I bet it has almost a full tank of gas.* He looked around and saw no one close by. He quickly put one of the jigglers into the key notch and jiggled. It didn't work. He tried a second time and then a third. Success! The driver's door was finally open. He got behind the wheel and closed the door. He took the screwdriver out of his pocket and stuck the head into the ignition and turned. The engine started. He was on his way out of the lot. Soon the Ford was running smoothly down Highway 41, going north back toward Adairsville. He had business to take care of there.

The boss had not answered or returned any of his calls since his scheme went sour, but he knew where to find him. It was the girl he really wanted. She was going to pay. He wanted her to squirm a while before he took care of her for good. Nobody got away with treating him like that. One woman had already learned that the hard way, and another would soon suffer the same kind of consequences.

When Houston got beyond Cartersville, he pulled into a QT gas station lot and parked his new Ford in one of the marked spaces. Then he took the girl's phone out of his left pocket. In her contacts, he found "Miss Riley." He touched the name to start the call.

"Hello?" the woman's voice on the line sounded a bit puzzled.

"Is this that meddlin' busybody of a Sunday school teacher they call Miss Riley?" he asked.

There was silence before Riley finally responded, "This is Riley Gordan."

"Your time is comin'," he said. "It may not be tomorrow or the next day, but it will be soon. Count on it. Your time is coming. You should never have interfered in my business." Houston discontinued the call, got out of the car, and dropped the phone in the litter basket on the sidewalk beside the store. After once again using the screwdriver to start the car, he drove out of the parking lot and continued north.

***

"You'll never guess who that was!" Riley said to Trish, standing in the middle of her living room with her phone still in hand and a shocked look on her face. "That was the man who kidnapped Kaylene. Houston, she called him. He just called to tell me 'my time is coming.'"

"Are you serious?" Trish raised her voice. "What are we going to do?"

"Well, the first thing I'm going to do is what I usually do in a crisis. I'm going down the hall to talk with Amos. He'll know how to handle this." Trish followed Riley to the Edwards' door.

"What's wrong?" Amos asked upon opening the door and seeing Riley's face.

Riley and Trish followed Amos inside, where Riley told him and Carol about the call.

"Are you sure it was him and not some buffoon who read the newspaper account playing a sick prank?" Amos asked.

"Oh, no. He used Kaylene's phone. Besides that, I recognized the voice, and he repeated the exact words he said in the motel parking lot— 'Your time is coming.' Those words were not recorded in the article."

"Then we need to call Charley," Amos insisted. His phone was already in his hand.

Chief Nelson was there with officer Jed in less than ten minutes.

He hardly took time to greet them before he was questioning Riley about the call. Once he was satisfied that he had learned all he could about the threat, he again quizzed Riley about the man's description. She couldn't think of anything other than what she had told him before.

He turned to Trish and asked, "Can you add anything to that, young lady?"

"Just look for the ugliest man in town," she told him. "I did notice he walked a little stooped and his chest was really hairy." Jed almost laughed but struggled to keep it to a grin. With Amos and Carol silently looking at her with puzzled expressions, Trish said, "Well, his shirt was unbuttoned."

"Until we're able to put this to rest, I'll have our patrols come by here regularly. Don't be alarmed if you see officers in a cruiser in your driveway in the middle of the night using their searchlights. If, at any time, you just think you might need us, call and we'll probably have someone here in six or seven minutes or less. Better to be cautious and bring us out for a false alarm than to be reluctant and allow something tragic to happen. I'm also going to pass this information on to Sheriff Langston since, technically, this is his case.

"I think I will make the Boyntons aware of this threat too. If this guy is after you, he may also be after Kaylene," Charlie told them before leaving.

Riley and Trish remained with Amos and Carol for a time after the Chief left. "Would you like to sleep in our guestroom tonight?" Carol asked Riley and Trish. "We've got plenty of room, and it could be a lot of fun."

Trish looked at Riley, but Riley shook her head. "No, I don't think so. I refuse to let an out-of-control maniac like this man control my life."

"I guess I'm with her," Trish told Carol.

They had coffee and some of Carol's freshly baked apple pie before returning to Riley's quarters down the hall. Once there they turned on the TV, but mostly talked. When both started yawning, they decided it was bedtime. "Could we leave the light on in here?" Trish asked.

"I don't see why not," Riley said. Secretly, she thought it was a great idea. "I can afford the extra power usage."

Riley was awakened shortly after one o'clock by Trish, who was standing in the entrance to her bedroom. "Riley," she spoke softly. "I heard a car drive into our driveway. A couple of minutes ago I heard noise out front like a car door closing. Someone is prowling around. Should we call the police?"

"Not yet," Riley said. "Let's investigate first. The car you heard was probably one of the patrolmen. Maybe the noise was a cat or something. Let's go down and check it out."

"Are you sure you want to do that?" Trish asked. "You know what the chief said about being cautious."

"I know, but we can't call the police every time we hear a noise. There are always noises in this building. Get your phone and something to use as a weapon."

Trish looked around and shrugged her shoulders. "I can't find a weapon."

"Here," Riley said, pulling a small, souvenir-type wooden baseball bat from beneath her bed. She gave it to Trish.

"You just happened to have a baseball bat stored under your bed?"

"It was a gift from my friend Davis Morgan," Riley told her.

"Why did Davis give you a bat?" Trish looked puzzled.

"It's a long story. You don't want to hear it tonight." They left the apartment with Trish taking her customary position three or four feet behind Riley. With phones as flashlights, the pair silently crept down the stairs that took them to the first floor. Riley put the key into the lock on the door to Kirby's apartment and turned it. The door opened. At almost precisely the same moment, the room was transformed from darkness to bright light. The girls squealed in unison. A man with a shocked expression on his face stood not more than six feet in front of them.

CHAPTER 12

"**I** didn't expect to get this kind of welcome in the middle of the night," the man said, smiling in the direction of his sister and her friend who had a baseball bat raised above her head.

"Kirby!" Riley ran toward her brother and hugged him. "What are you doing here?" she asked, still holding on to him.

"This is where I live," he told her.

"Yes, it is, and I'm so glad you're home. I've missed you."

"I would have made it for dinner if a little car trouble hadn't slowed me down."

"I thought the plan was for you to be here next week?"

"It was, but as it turned out, they settled the case. There was no need for me to testify, so I didn't need to stick around. I thought I might as well get on up here and see my little sister."

"I doubt it was your sister you were so anxious to see. I think it was probably that girl you hang around with when you're here, who, incidentally, can't wait to get a look at you." Riley glanced toward Trish who was standing silently, still holding her phone in one hand and the bat in the other. "I'm sure you remember my friend Trish."

Trish put the bat in the same hand as her phone and waved with her free hand while flashing a smile. "Don't mind me. I'm just standing over here letting my heart rate settle back down," she explained.

They visited for a few minutes without Riley mentioning the recent unpleasantness. Kirby didn't bring it up, and Riley was glad. They could talk about that later. "My car is loaded with my junk, most of which I will unload tomorrow, after I've gotten some sleep. But if you girls will excuse me, I do need a couple of things tonight."

"Of course," Riley said. "And we need to get back to our beauty sleep."

"Yes, and some of us need it more than others," Trish said, looking at Riley, who appeared gloriously glamorous even after getting out of bed in the middle of the night. "Let's go back to bed. I think I can sleep now that we have Kirby standing guard down here."

The last statement prompted Kirby to look toward Riley as if he wanted an explanation, but none was given. "Good night, sweet brother," Riley said, kissing him on the forehead. "I hope you sleep well for what's left of the night."

After returning to her bed, it took Riley a while to get back to sleep. *Kirby seems so happy now. For so long he never smiled. He's been through more than any human being ought to have to endure; losing Sherrie to someone else who happened to be his best friend and then her death, cut from the Royals organization, losing Mom and Dad so unexpectedly. It all hit him at once. I wondered if he would ever bounce back.* She thanked God for the two factors that she knew had turned her brother around. Most important was the renewal of his spiritual life over the past year. Kirby had never been a bad person, but for a time he seemed to try to live his life without God's input. That was now changing in a marvelous way. The second component was Connie Reece. Kirby had never told Riley, but she had no doubt that her brother was hopelessly in love with Connie. Nothing produces happiness like love! When Riley finally fell asleep, she rested well for the remainder of the night.

***

Kirby drove out of his driveway at precisely 8:30. He thought about leaving earlier but didn't want to arrive at Connie's office ahead of her. He saw her car parked in a space on the street. He felt his pulse rate surge. He had not seen her in several weeks. He practically ran up the stairs, but slowed his pace before walking through the office door.

Connie was looking down at something on her desk. She looked up when he came through the door. For a split second she sat there as if in disbelief. Then, bouncing out of her chair, she made a sound that was a strange combination of a shriek and his name. "Kirby! I don't believe it. You're here." She ran in his direction. He greeted her with outstretched arms. They embraced. A long kiss followed. It was even better than what he had anticipated on his drive from Florida.

"Why? How? I thought it would be at least another week before you got home. How did you manage this?"

"I couldn't wait any longer to see my girl, so I just packed up and came home," he told her.

"Why didn't you let me know when you were going to get here? I could have prepared."

"What were you going to do, bake a cake? I wanted to surprise you. The greeting is always better when it's a surprise."

"Surprise or not, I'm thrilled to have you home." They kissed again. "This is a business office," Connie reminded him, displaying the beautiful smile he had come to love. "I guess we'd better act like it." Connie returned to her chair behind the desk. Kirby settled into the chair nearby. For a few minutes the couple's conversation was typical of two people in love who had not seen each other for several weeks. Each talked of how much the other had been missed. They spoke of how they had tried to fill their time with the other being absent.

"What kind of mess is this that my sister has gotten herself into?" Kirby asked after a few minutes.

Connie told him as much of the story as she knew, including the account of the recent threat Riley had received. "I'm thrilled to have you home, but I'm glad especially for Riley's sake that you're here. What I've heard of the kidnapper causes me to believe he's some kind of depraved monster. I fear for Riley's life."

"We won't let that happen," Kirby told her, but there was concern in his voice. Before leaving, Kirby asked her to have dinner with him. Connie gladly accepted the invitation. Kirby left the office a happy man. It was good to be home.

Instead of getting into his car, Kirby walked up the street to the police headquarters to see his good friend, Charley Nelson. He had worked with Charley as a consultant on a couple of cases last summer and fall while on rehab leave in Adairsville. The chief might be willing to talk with him about what he knew of the kidnapping case.

"Well, if it isn't the big city detective!" Charley greeted him when he entered the chief's office. "Is this a visit or have you returned permanently?"

"I guess it's permanent since I no longer have a job. Going to give business a try," he declared.

"So, do we have the same arrangement as last summer? If I need you, I call you, and compensate you with peanuts."

"Sounds good to me. I might as well use all this training I have, and being an old ballplayer, I've always liked peanuts. I won't keep you from your work. I wondered if you could enlighten me about this ordeal that Riley got herself involved in?"

"There's not a lot I can tell you. You know that the sheriff and GBI are handling the case. I've asked them to keep me in the loop. So far, they've been obliging." The chief told him pretty much the same story he had heard from Amos, starting with the kidnapping and going through Riley's rescue of the girl. He also spoke of the telephone threat. "There are two recent developments, I learned late yesterday," he told Kirby. "I don't see any reason to withhold them from you."

"I would appreciate knowing all there is to know. I think you understand my concern for my sister. She's all the family I have left, and as you know, we are extremely close. I don't want to get in anyone's way, but I will protect her till my last breath."

"A woman's body was found in the Altoona area earlier in the week. Late yesterday, we got word that her fingerprints match prints found on some of the things left behind in the motel when the kidnappers fled. She had been beaten to death."

"So, apparently, her brutal death was payback for her role in allowing the kid to escape," Kirby speculated.

"Gives us a pretty good idea of the kind of beast we're up against, doesn't it?" Charley commented. "The second development is that the green metallic Kia Soul they used was found in Marietta yesterday. It had a different license plate number than the one given by the kidnapper for motel registration, but he, no doubt, gave an incorrect number to hide the fact it was stolen. What clerk goes out and checks the plate number? It's definitely the car, right down to the taillight Riley smashed. Another car was stolen a few blocks from where that one was left."

"Do you know the model of that one?"

"It was a white Ford Taurus."

"And do you have any information about where the abandoned one was originally stolen?" Kirby inquired.

"It had a Bibb County license plate. That's the county in which Macon is located. I figure there're still two people to be apprehended. The one who did the kidnapping and the one that put him up to it. It appears this was all about getting Nate Bannister out of the special election. I can't imagine the thug Riley and Kaylene told us about had a personal reason to do that. He was just a hired gun."

"You're probably right, but he's the loose cannon that concerns me. He's the one who is out to get my sister. Do you have any ideas about the identity of the guy calling the shots?"

"To early to speculate about that," Charley told him. "Incidentally, I hope to get a profile of the murdered woman sometime in the next few days. Perhaps that will help us identify the killer. In the meantime, we are keeping a close watch on your place. You might warn Riley about being out and about too much."

"I'll do that, but you know Riley. She doesn't always respond well to instructions—or even suggestions."

After leaving the police station, Kirby visited with Davis Morgan at the bookshop. Afterwards he had a sandwich at the Mattie Mae Tea Room in the same building. Upon returning to the compound that was home, he sat in his car and admired the beautifully renovated church building that now served as a living space. *Uncle James never wasted a good idea, and this was one of his best.*

Having not yet seen Amos and Carol, he went to their apartment. The couple he had grown to love over the past year were as glad to see him as he was to greet them. They had just finished lunch; Carol scolded him for eating earlier. She did manage to talk him into a piece of pie. It was hard to get away from the Edwards' home without eating something. They chatted for a few minutes before he left to confront Riley about her recent troubles. It had to be done. He found her and Trish at the table munching on sandwiches.

"I bet I know where you went first thing this morning," Riley declared.

"Yeah, I went to our office. Got to stay on top of business matters, you know," Kirby said with a straight face.

"Business my eye. I know the reason you went there, and it had nothing to do with business. Was she glad to see you?" Riley asked.

"She said she was, and she acted as if she was. I guess she was glad to see me. I know I was delighted to see her." He turned to Trish. "Has Riley shown you the sights since you've been here?"

"Sure, we've seen a dilapidated house that no one has lived in for twenty years, an old school that hasn't seen students in forty years, and an abandoned factory building that has held no machinery since the first Mr. Bush was president. We've seen it all."

"Now Trish, it hasn't been that bad. We spent an afternoon on Chatsworth Mountain, one of the prettiest places in north Georgia, and we went to the mall," Riley reminded her.

"Oh yes, the mall. I forgot about the mall. That's what I drove all the way down here to see. We don't have malls up where I live, you know."

"Well, I promise you that after the next few days, you're going to know as much about our area as most natives. We're going to see the sights."

"From what Chief Nelson tells me, you might want to put a hold on that," Kirby suggested.

"Oh, you saw him too," Riley mumbled.

"Yes, I did, and I talked with him about some things we need to talk about after you're through with your lunch."

Kirby and Trish chatted as Riley nibbled, obviously trying to make her lunch last as long as possible. When she finally took the last bite of her sandwich, Trish spoke up. "Why don't you two go into the sitting room? I'll clean up here. I know you have brother–sister things to talk about." She gave Riley a mocking smile. Riley stuck her tongue out at her.

Kirby followed his sister into her living room. "Riley, I want to know everything about this ordeal with the kidnapper. Start at the beginning and tell me everything."

Riley began her account by saying, "You know I didn't go out looking for this. It just sort of fell into my lap."

"I know," Kirby responded. "No one is blaming you. Your heart was right, and you probably saved a little girl's life, but now you're in danger and we need to take precautions to protect you. Tell me what happened."

Riley told her story just as Kirby had heard it from the others.

It's her empathy that gets her into such messes, Kirby decided. *Most people stand outside and watch, but because she cares, she jumps in with both feet. I'm glad I have a kindhearted sister, but it sure keeps me busy.* "I've learned from my involvement in sports that sometimes the best defense is a good offense. Maybe I need to approach this by going after your nemesis, Houston, as well as whoever put him up to his meanness," Kirby reasoned.

Riley reached over to a nearby table to pick up a small stack of file folders and handed them to Kirby. "This is the research I asked Connie to do. There might be a suspect in there somewhere. I'll give them to you and let you go through them with a fine-tooth comb. There are three possibilities that jump out at me."

"Who are those?" Kirby asked, shooting a glance at Trish as she hurried through on her way to the guest room.

"Not necessarily in order of probability, there is Kenneth Cotes. Mr. Cotes is a contractor. Actually, his three sons are gradually assuming more and more of the responsibility, but he is the owner. He also owns part interest in a fitness center and restaurant, both located in Cartersville. There are two reasons I think he's a suspect. First, he's the contractor that stands to make some real money if the Outdoor

Sportsman store, which Nate Bannister opposes, is built here. Secondly, he thinks Nate Bannister shot his dog. For years he has declared that he will get even."

"That makes sense," Kirby remarked. "Who is your second suspect?"

"As I see it, a man named Jason Purcell is a possibility. He's from Macon, and a representative of the Outdoor Sportsman. When he showed up at Amos and Carol's for dinner recently, he warned that we should campaign against Nate Bannister. According to 'Mr. Slick,' we will lose a lot of money if he's elected. I'm sure either Amos or Connie has told you that his company wants to buy property we own out beside the interstate. You can expect him to contact you some time soon."

"Sounds like you're not too fond of Mr. Purcell," Kirby suggested.

"I don't know that he's our man, but I was not favorably impressed with him. Too slick for my taste. The third man that interests me is Edward Neff. I don't know of any business conflicts with Nate, but he and his family have been carrying on a running feud with him. It seems that years ago, his now deceased father was seriously injured in an accident with Nate. The family has never forgotten it. When I recently went into Edward's convenience store, he still seemed pretty bitter. He had nothing good to say about Nate Bannister."

"Who's running against Nate?" Kirby asked.

"It's an ambitious man by the name of Randy Tate. He is progressive as a politician, while Nate is conservative, but his character seems to be beyond reproach. Even those that disagree with him seem to respect him as a person."

"Well, you and Connie have done a good job of giving me something to start with. I think I would like to meet each of these guys."

"Is it okay for me to come back in there?" Trish stuck her head through the doorway. "Are the fireworks over?"

"We would enjoy having you join us, Trish. There never were any fireworks," Kirby told her.

CHAPTER 13

"I missed all the greenness of everything while away from this region," Kirby remarked, looking around at the landscape. He and Connie had gone to Cartersville for an early dinner. As they left, he noticed the beautiful sunset in the west.

"Yeah, but you had Disney World and beaches where you've been the last few months," Connie remarked.

"I've never been to Disney World and was seldom on a beach while down there. I did occasionally take a late afternoon stroll along the shore. I didn't do so very often because it caused me to miss you so much."

"Oh, that's sweet, but, you know, you could have sent for me, and we could've taken those walks together."

"We'll do that sometime in the near future," Kirby promised. "I'd love to introduce you to some of my Florida friends. You would love Ken and Eva Pate and little Charlotte. I got to know them at the church I attended there."

They drove for a few more minutes before arriving back in Adairsville. Kirby turned off Highway 41, which took them toward Maple Grove Drive, where Connie lived with her mother.

A car was stopped in the road up ahead. A man signaled for them to stop. Kirby pulled as far off the road as he could. He got out and strolled over to where the man stood beside the car. "Can I help you, sir?" he asked.

"Yeah, I seem to have run out of gas," the man said. "Do you think you might be able to find a gas can and bring some back to me?"

Connie had the door on her side of the car open, listening to the conversation. "Kirby, I have a full two-gallon gas can in my garage at home. We can use that and replace it before I do any mowing tomorrow."

"Great," Kirby responded. "Sir, we'll be back in a flash. It's only a couple of streets over."

He hopped back into the car. In a minute or two they were in Connie's driveway. She opened the garage door and pointed to the red can. Kirby put it in the trunk of his car, and in a couple of minutes they were back where they left the man. Kirby poured gas from the can into the tank, then placed the can back into the trunk and waited to see if the man's car would start. It turned over but didn't immediately start. Finally, the motor was running. The man rolled down his window and shouted, "Thanks," before driving away.

"I guess he forgot," Kirby remarked to Connie as the car was disappearing around the curve.

"What did he forget?" Connie asked.

"He forgot to offer to pay us for the gas."

"Maybe he didn't have the money," Connie suggested. "He didn't look well-to-do."

"Maybe so, but he could at least have given some explanation. That's just common courtesy."

As they returned to Connie's house, Kirby continued to mull over their experience with the stranded stranger. There was something that wasn't registering. It came to him like a bolt of lightning just before pulling into Connie's drive. "No!" he cried. "It couldn't be!"

"What are you talking about?" Connie asked.

"I'm talking about the man who ran out of gas! That was a Ford Taurus he was driving, wasn't it?"

"I think so," Connie replied.

"Did you notice the county on the license plate?"

"I think it was Cobb County. Why? Is that important?"

"Isn't that the county where Marietta is located?" he asked. "According to Charley, the kidnapper probably recently stole a white

Ford Taurus from a lot in Marietta. Don't you think that man we just helped pretty well fit the description Riley gave of the kidnapper?"

"Could be," Connie said after thinking about it for a moment. "But that seems pretty far-fetched. I know coincidences happen, but that would be too much."

"Not necessarily," Kirby insisted. "This is a small town. I think there is a good chance it was him. I may have had him and let him off the hook," Kirby groaned. "He's going to have to get some more gas. Those two gallons won't take him far. Let's take a quick tour of the gas stations out near the interstate and see if we can catch him. I definitely have some questions for him."

They drove through the parking lots of six stations on Highway 140 near the interstate exit but saw no white Ford Taurus. "He's still in town somewhere, or else he took off up or down I-75 and plans to get his fuel at a station there. I could kick myself! Some detective I am," he moaned.

***

The well-groomed man was driving north on I-75 when his phone rang. He pulled it out of his pocket and looked at it. It was Houston again. *I guess I ought to take it and get it over with*, he decided, answering the call. "Hang on a minute, I'm on the highway. There's a ramp just ahead."

He pulled into a truck stop. "So, what do you need, Houston?"

"To begin with, I need some money. This car I'm drivin' won't run without gas, and I haven't had anything to eat since yesterday. You owe me, and I aim to collect."

"I don't owe you a penny. If anything, you owe me. I gave you advance money to do a job for me with the promise of more when the job was completed. You botched it. The old man is still on the ballot. You finish the job, and I'll give you the rest of the money."

"I'll do that right after I take care of that meddlesome Gordan girl. I owe her big time."

"You leave her alone and do your job. She has a brother who, I think, is back in town now and will eat you alive."

"I'll do my job, but she's goin' to get what's comin' to her. In the meantime, I need some money to live on."

"It goes against my better judgment, but if you promise me you won't waste any more time in taking Bannister out of the picture, I'll advance you three hundred more dollars. That's it. That's all you get from me until you do the work you agreed to."

"I could use more, but I guess three hundred is better than nothin', but I need it now. I mean right now! I'm almost out of gas and I'm starvin'. I could also use a place to sleep."

"Where are you?" the man asked.

"I'm sitting on a little farm or logging road that runs off of Highway 140 just past Hampton Inn."

"Do you have enough gas to get to the next exit going south on I-75?"

"I can probably get there, but that's just about the limit."

"Okay, take that exit, the White Road exit, and you'll find truck stops on both sides of the road. Pull into the one on the left as you drive east and look for my rental car. It's a black Chevrolet Malibu. I'll be waiting for you with your money, but I'm giving you twenty minutes. I plan to be out of here after that, so don't waste any time in getting here."

I must've been out of my mind to hook up with a clod like that. I hope he can find his way here. I'm going to have to play along with him or find a way to permanently get rid of him. He knows enough to put me away for a long time.

***

Trish had gone to the outlet mall in Calhoun, hoping to find just the right outfit to wear for her date with Nathan that evening. Meanwhile, Riley, Kirby, and Amos decided to meet in the beautiful downstairs study. It was built around the stained-glass window where the church pulpit once stood and was their favorite place for meetings. Connie, as their business administrator, had made the less than five-minute trip from the Reece home to also be there. She was counting on it being a short meeting, as Kirby had promised. It was Saturday and she had things to do at home. Riley had prepared the coffee maker earlier. Each of the four people either had a cup in hand or one on a nearby piece of furniture.

Amos reminded them that, on Monday, the Cleaning Crew—Bill, Jessie, and Juan—would be shifting gears a bit for a few days. Under his supervision, they would be tearing down the old, abandoned house. "It's a small-frame house built with crawl space. So, rather than takin' equipment out for demolition, I plan to equip the guys with sledgehammers and crowbars and let them at it. We can pile the remains, and I know a fellow who'll haul it all away. He'll want to salvage some of the material, if it's worth it."

"Sounds like a plan to me. You make sure you stick to supervising, Amos. Carol will have our hides if she finds you out there swinging a sledgehammer," Kirby commented.

"I'll let the boys do the heavy stuff," Amos promised. "They're good workers and probably wouldn't want an old man getting in their way."

"While in Florida, I thought a lot about those guys," Kirby stated. "Connie, you handle the books, how are they progressing? Are we anywhere near being in the black with the cleaning business?"

"We're very close. Two out of the last four months showed a profit with the other two months just falling short. They continue to pick up customers. It has steadily grown from the time we started it a year ago."

"Here's my idea," Kirby said. "We didn't start the cleaning business because we needed any profit it might provide. It was born out of two concerns. First, it was to give our three friends jobs that would provide them a paycheck. Secondly, we needed to spruce up our apartments and rental houses between occupants, as well as do a bit of maintenance. Why can't we eliminate a little of our own workload by giving the company to the guys, and signing a contract with them to take care of our work? The money from our agreement, along with the contracts they have with outside establishments, should provide nicely for them. I suspect putting everything in their hands would motivate them to seek new business and provide an opportunity for them to develop business skills. What do you think? Am I off base?"

Everyone looked toward Amos. "It sounds like a good thing for us and the boys," he surmised. "How about the building they work out of? Would we continue to hold the title and rent it to them or give it to them outright?"

"We can do whatever you guys decide, but I had in mind turning the building, the equipment, and even the two vehicles over to them," Kirby said. "What need do we have for that stuff, other than for the Cleaning Crew? Let's give them the best opportunity to succeed."

"The whole idea sounds perfect to me," Riley chimed in. "Because we want the crew to succeed, maybe it could best be accomplished a step at a time over the next couple of years. It might not be good to throw them in immediately to sink or swim. Maybe they could be eased into it, fully informed of the ultimate goal." At that point Max, having followed them into the study, jumped into Riley's lap. She welcomed him by stoking his head.

"That sounds reasonable. What kind of schedule do you have in mind?" Amos asked.

"Oh, I don't know," Riley responded, still rubbing Max's head. "Maybe instead of a salary, we could go ahead and start paying according to profit earned. That would be motivation for finding new customers. Then maybe after, say, six months, we could turn the books over to them. If everything is still solid after another year, we sign it over to them."

"Do you think they are ready for something like that?" Kirby asked Amos.

"I do. They've come a long way in the last year. They are loyal, honest, and hard workers, who are well on the road to becoming fine family men. I like Riley's idea of taking it a step at a time. It takes a lot of the pressure off them, but at the same time offers incentive."

"Connie, you haven't expressed your opinion. How do you feel about this proposal?"

"I think I work for the most wonderful people in the world," she replied. "I don't know of anyone else who would even consider giving a company away just as it starts earning a profit. If Bill, Juan, and Jessie are good with it, then let's do it."

"Thank you, Connie. It comes into perspective when you remember that all of this was given to us," Kirby reminded her. "And we're pretty lucky to have you working with us." He smiled in her direction.

"Come on. This is a business meeting. You two can do your courting some other time," Riley suggested with a giggle.

"Okay. Amos and Riley will work on a timeline for turning the cleaning business over to the Cleaning Crew. Then Amos can talk with them about our plans. Are we all in agreement with that?" Kirby asked. Everyone nodded.

They talked briefly of several other concerns, including the hiring of a manager for the hardware store in Canton, which would require one of them to make the short trip there sometime in the next week or so. "Having the right person in place to manage those stores is extremely important since they are located too far away for us to keep a close eye on them," Connie reminded them.

"There is one other item I want to mention that has nothing to do with business," Kirby said. "I'm concerned about the threat Riley received from the kidnapper. It may be a bluff for the purpose of making her miserable for a while, but there is also the possibility that he intends to do what he is threatening. Last night Connie and I had a brief encounter with a man who very well could have been that thug. We saw him about five minutes from here. I've informed our police department and the sheriff, but let's keep our eyes open. The quicker he's behind bars, the quicker we can get on with business. I don't think I have to tell you that if you spot anyone who is suspicious, you need to call the authorities. Connie has yard work to do, so we will dismiss this meeting and let her get to it."

***

Mike had Saturday evening duty, so Riley spent the evening at home alone reading, with Max in her lap much of the time. Trish returned a little before eleven from her evening in Rome with Nathan. They had gone there for dinner and a little theater production.

"How was your date?" Riley asked.

"I think I'm in love," Trish replied, looking dreamy-eyed. "Nathan is one of the kindest and most considerate guys I've known. Did you know he has his Master of Divinity degree and is already working on a PhD?" Without giving Riley opportunity to answer her question, she continued, "He plans to continue to minister to teens for a few years, and then he would like to be a college or seminary professor. I think he'll make a great teacher."

"Sounds like you had a fabulous evening. I'm glad it worked out."

"He kissed me on the cheek after walking me to the door. I know it was just a peck on the cheek, but it was a start. I think he really likes me," Trish excitedly proclaimed. "The senior pastor of his church is out of town, and Nathan is speaking tomorrow. I know you've got to teach your class, but do you think it would be okay for me to go and hear him speak? I think he really wants me there."

"Sure, there's no reason you can't do that. I wish it were possible for me to go with you, but it's a little late for me to find someone to sub in my class. Kaylene will probably be back, so I think it's sort of important I be there."

"I wouldn't want you to snub your responsibility to the Lord for the sake of my love life. I don't mind going alone."

Later in the evening, as Riley lay in bed, she pondered Trish's excitement about the evening. She was with Trish almost constantly through four years of college. She didn't remember her ever showing such enthusiasm for any guy. She was glad Trish and Nathan seemed to be fond of each other, but she hoped she had not set her friend up for heartbreak. After two or three minutes, Riley asked herself, *Why do I do that? It's going well for the two of them and all I can think about is, what if their relationship turns out to be a disappointment? Why can't I have a positive attitude about such matters?*

When Riley finally got to sleep, she had a dream that she had experienced at other times over the past five years. She vividly saw a large jet dropping toward the ocean. She heard a woman's scream. The nose of the aircraft hit the water, and it disappeared completely. Then there was only silence. She awoke in a cold sweat. She slept little for the remainder of the night. Some of her awake time was used to pray for Nathan and Trish's relationship. Then those prayers turned to her own relationship with Mike.

CHAPTER 14

Riley rode to church with Amos and Carol. Trish had left a half hour earlier for her trip to Calhoun. Kirby drove by the Reece house to chauffeur Connie and Beth to the service. The Boynton's were back at church, and Kaylene seemed no worse for wear considering her recent ordeal. She was the center of attention in the middle school department. Whether or not she knew the answers, her hand was usually the first to go up when Riley asked a question. It was good to have things back to normal.

Nate was sitting with the Boyntons when the Sunday school crowd entered the auditorium after class. Across the aisle, Riley was seated with Amos and Carol. She noticed that every time someone entered, Nate turned to thoroughly scrutinize them. She wondered if he had that big gun under his jacket. The thought caused her a little uneasiness. As usual, Pastor Jensen brought a lively and informative message. He spoke of the children of Israel's triumph at Jericho, pointing out that their victory was possible because they followed God's specific instructions. "That's still how victory is found," he told them.

After church, Kirby went home with Beth and Connie for lunch. Riley was helping Carol in the kitchen and Amos was in the living room getting started on the Sunday paper when Trish came in. She was raving about Nathan's sermon.

While they all feasted on Carol's roast beef with all the trimmings, as she would say, they got a blow-by-blow account of the youth pastor's message. That was followed by a fashion review, as Trish described the suit and shirt he wore. She revealed that his tie was just right, and his shoes well-polished.

"I think she likes the guy," Amos remarked.

After lunch, Riley and Trish helped Carol clean up the kitchen. Amos returned to his paper but was dozing in his recliner with his paper lying across his face when the ladies got to the living room.

"Mike on duty today?" Carol asked Riley.

"No, he worked last night," Riley replied. "He didn't want to miss Nathan's sermon this morning, so he went to church almost directly from work. He will get three or four hours sleep this afternoon before coming by here later. Then it's back on duty at ten o'clock. He's got a couple of days off after that."

"Seems like his work schedule jumps all over the place," Carol remarked.

"Most of the guys on the force are married with families. I think, since Mike has more flexibility, Charley plugs him in wherever he's needed. Mike doesn't seem to care. He just shows up when he's told and does his job."

"Sounds like the chief's taking advantage of Mike's good-natured disposition," Trish said matter-of-factly.

"Maybe he is. Maybe a lot of us are doing that," Riley said with a distant look on her face.

Trish looked closely at her but offered no response.

Amos came alive and lifted his head from under his paper. "We're enjoying having you here with us, Trish. How much longer will we have that honor?"

"Are you ready for me to go, Amos? Are you hinting that I need to be on my way?"

"Not at all," he responded. "I love having as many beautiful women as possible around, and I've surely been blessed these past couple of weeks with attractive ladies wherever I look."

"You're quick, Amos, I'll give you that. You're the man with the silver tongue," Trish laughed. "I'd planned to go on down to Florida this Friday, but now I don't know. I may stay a few more days. It just sort of depends on how things go, and how much longer Riley will agree to put up with me."

"I'd love for you to move in permanently," Riley responded.

"You'd better be careful with such statements. You'd be shocked if I took you up on it."

***

"Do you know Randy Tate, the man running against Nate Bannister?" Kirby asked Connie while they were comfortably seated on the Reece sofa after lunch. Beth was still busy in the kitchen but had shooed them out.

"You just can't stop playing detective, can you?" she scolded.

"I'm not playing detective. I'm trying to get some information. Tell me what you know about him."

"Well, he's a middle-aged man who has held a couple of different Bartow County political positions in the past. I think, maybe, he lost at least one election. He makes his living running an insurance agency. I've met him, but don't really know him well."

"Do he and Nate have any history?" Kirby asked.

"Not that I know about," Connie told him. "I don't think he grew up in Cartersville. If I remember the facts from the research I did for Riley correctly, he came here as a young adult, maybe thirty years ago."

"Where was he originally from?" Kirby quickly asked.

"Now you are really testing my memory. You'd better check this out in the files I gave your sister, but maybe he came here from the central part of the state, perhaps Crawford County. Yes, I believe it was Crawford County." She now sounded surer of her information.

"You've got to remember I grew up in New England. I don't have any idea where Crawford County is."

"If I remember my Georgia geography correctly, it's a small county that borders Bibb County, which is where Macon is located," Connie explained.

"What was your impression of the man on those occasions when you were around him?" Kirby asked.

"I don't know that he ever made an impression on me one way or the other. To be honest, I remember very little about him."

"I've got an appointment to meet him tomorrow. With him running for office, I've an excuse to do so. I'm to meet with Purcell on Tuesday, and that was easy enough to arrange, since he is anxious to talk with me about the property his company is interested in. I'm trying to figure out how to best arrange sessions with Neff and Cotes without them becoming suspicious of my intentions," Kirby said.

"And it's not hard to figure out your intent. Those, no doubt, are the four people you have pegged as suspects behind Kaylene's abduction."

"I don't know if I would call any of them suspects, but they are all I've got at this time," Kirby explained.

"Why do you even have to worry with this? Why can't you just leave it to the authorities? That's why we have them."

"It's not like I'm looking for a mystery to occupy my time. I don't need to be constantly working on a case. I'm trying to protect my sister. I do have some experience in dealing with crime, and I might as well put it to use."

"You don't fool me for one minute, Kirby Gordan. You flourish in the midst of an unsolved mystery. You're convinced you're another Sherlock Holmes or Father Brown. I just don't want you to get hurt. Why, you're not even licensed to carry a gun in this state. What if that Houston guy comes at you with his gun? What're you goin' to do then?"

"This coming from the girl who was with Riley, searching an old house in the woods after dark. If I've learned anything in law enforcement, it's how to protect myself from such situations. Don't worry. I'll be fine."

Beth Reece walked into the room. "What situation are you talking about?" she asked.

"It's nothing for you to worry about, Mom," Connie told her. "It doesn't concern you. It's something we can work out."

"I know, don't bother with me. I'm just a demented old lady who doesn't have the capacity to comprehend a normal conversation," Beth replied, seating herself in her favorite chair.

"Oh, Mom, don't be so touchy," Connie told her.

"You're not demented, and you're not an old lady, Mrs. Reece," Kirby insisted. "You're one of the most beautiful, smart, and mature ladies I know. That's one of the reasons I'm attracted to your daughter. I figure she will be just as beautiful and brilliant as you when she reaches your age."

"And not near as sassy," Connie muttered.

"Kirby, you've been hanging around that old flirt Amos Edwards too long. You're starting to sound just like him, but thanks for the compliment anyway." Beth smiled in his direction.

Kirby remained with the Reece ladies for almost another hour before driving home to turn on his TV to watch the last few innings of a Braves game. He had finally reached the point of enjoying baseball again. For so long, after he was cut by the Royals, he could not even sit and watch a game without becoming sad and depressed. He was glad that had passed.

His mind went to Connie. He had decided during the weeks they were separated that he definitely loved her and wanted to spend the remainder of his life with her. Before he popped the question, he would need to purchase a ring. He had done the ring thing once before. His mind focused for a moment on Sherrie. There was a flash of ecstasy that immediately turned to sadness. It had been several years since their life together ended. The tragic conclusion of her time on this earth came a year ago, but she still had a way of forcing her way into his thoughts. He decided he would get Amos's help with the ring. He would know where to go and what to look for. Kirby knew he leaned too heavily on Amos. *He's reaching the age where he deserves a little rest and relaxation, and I need to respect that. I will start doing so after I have a ring for Connie,* he decided. *He'll love helping out with that.*

***

Houston, not being overly familiar with Adairsville, drove around for a while just outside of town, looking for a place to park his car where it would be out of sight. He found a logging road running off Mostellers

Mill Road. It was little more than a trail and seemed to fit the bill. He could live in his car for a short time. He had done it before. He reached for a bag of food and a pint of booze bought with the money the boss gave him. That should hold him until dark. He needed darkness for the next part of his plan.

After pondering it for a while, he had decided to blow the old man away first. By doing that, he would get his payoff from the boss quicker. Then he could take care of the girl whenever and however he chose. The only problem was that he needed a rifle. He wasn't about to approach that crazy old man and his gun up close. He needed a rifle to ambush the dude. But that shouldn't be a problem. This was north Georgia. He guessed there was a rifle and ammo in about three out of every four houses. He would wait until dark, pick out a house where it appeared no one was home, walk in, locate what he needed, and walk out. No real risk. He had observed that the Adairsville cops heavily patrolled the neighborhoods within the city limits, but he doubted that any law would be haunting the county roads tonight.

While waiting, Houston occasionally took a sip from the bottle. His mind was on the boss. He wasn't sure he trusted him. *If I didn't need the money so badly, I'd be out of here. He'd better think twice about trying to cheat me out of what's mine. He talks big, but he had to hire me to do the real work. Not man enough to do it himself.*

With the liquor taking effect, combined with the heat in the car despite the open windows, Houston began to feel drowsy. Soon he was dozing, and then sound asleep. It was two hours into darkness before he awoke. He sat up straight, stretched, and then picked up the almost empty bottle to finish it off. He threw the bottle through the open window, started the car with his screwdriver, and drove out of the woods to the road. He looked for the right location to accomplish his mission. There was a medium-sized brick house sitting off the road to his left. It was isolated, with no lights on or any other signs of life. *Looks like the place*, he decided.

He parked the car and got out. He used the butt of his gun to break the glass in the door, then reached through the broken pane to unlock it. Then he was on the inside, walking through the front room, barely able to see by the security light shining in from the outside. He went through a door to his left and found a light switch. He flipped it and the room was immediately filled with light. It looked like a den or, perhaps, family room. Sure enough, there it was, a gun rack. In a couple of minutes, he had his rifle and ammo. He decided to look around for anything else worth taking with him. He pulled out a couple of drawers looking for cash but found none. Then, through a window, he saw the blue lights of a police car pulling into the long drive. He ran out of the house and toward his car. The police car stopped. Two officers popped out.

"Adairsville police. Stop and drop your weapon, or I'll shoot," one of the officers called out.

Quick as a flash, without even thinking or aiming, Houston slightly raised the rifle and fired.

***

It was hardly past 10:30 when the call came in. A resident of a home on Mostellers Mill Road reported that he and his wife were upstairs in bed. They had just heard glass breaking and the sound of someone walking around downstairs. Evidently, they had a burglar! The dispatcher successfully reached officers who were patrolling in a development not far from that location. "I guess it's not going to be a boring evening after all," Jed said to Mike. "A half hour into our shift and already a prowler call."

"Probably the family cat. That's the way these alarms usually turn out," Mike retorted, stepping on the accelerator to speed in the direction of Mostellers Mill Road. They were there in less than five minutes. Their flashing blue lights seemed to disturb the serene setting as they passed the Pleasant Valley Baptist Church with the cemetery on the opposite side of the road.

"That's it!" Jed called out as they approached a long drive leading to a brick house they could see in the distance. Mike slowed the car to pull in. A white Ford Taurus sat in the drive. Mike brought the cruiser to a standstill well behind the white vehicle. "I guess we'd better check it out," Jed said before opening the passenger door to bounce out of the car. Mike was out and on his feet only moments after his partner. It was then that the officers saw the man with a rifle running from the front door toward the white car.

"Adairsville police. Stop and drop your weapon, or I'll shoot," Mike yelled, drawing his service revolver. Before either man could react, the thief fired. One of the officers immediately dropped to the ground. The other fired, but his shot bounced off the car as the target was leaping into the driver's seat. The engine was running. The car swung through the yard wide of the police cruiser. The officer still on his feet took three desperation shots at the vehicle as it passed, but none of them halted the fugitive who was soon on the road and out of sight.

The officer ran toward his fallen partner. He fell to the ground on his knees beside him. Blood covered the area just under his right arm. The officer called his friend's name, but the only response was an unintelligible mumble. He was quickly on the radio attached to the shoulder of his uniform. "Officer down at 404 Mostellers Mill Road near Pleasant Valley Baptist Church. I need help. I need an ambulance. Hurry, it's critical."

A couple wearing pajamas came from the house. "What can we do?" the man asked the officer on his knees, but there was no reply. The officer compressed the wound of his partner. Soon the yard was filled with people in uniform. He let go of his wounded friend only when the medics insisted. They gently cared for the injury and loaded the wounded officer onto the stretcher before rapidly driving away. Chief Nelson helped the distraught officer to his feet and led him to the steps to the porch. He helped him sit and then sat beside him with his right arm around his shoulder. The veteran officer began to weep as the chief held him.

CHAPTER 15

It was almost eleven-thirty when Riley crawled in bed and turned off the lamp on the stand beside her. She was thinking of Mike. Nathan had come by after finishing his Sunday evening duties at church. He and Trish had gone out for an evening snack. That left her and Mike alone for a while. She enjoyed that hour. She realized that they had seldom had alone time in the year she had known him. Though they were together a lot, it was seldom just the two of them. They were usually at some event or with another couple. Their dates were almost always group events. It occurred to her that she, not Mike, was responsible for that. It wasn't that she feared Mike would be anything other than the perfect gentleman. She knew she could count on him to act like the Christian he was. Why then had she always maneuvered the situation in that direction?

The phone she had laid on the stand beside the lamp rang. *Must be Kirby. Only he would call this late.* She picked up the phone without turning on the light. "Hello," she said. "This is Riley."

She didn't immediately recognize the voice on the line. "I apologize for calling at this time of the night, but I knew you would want to know."

She realized it was Charley Nelson. *What does he have to tell me that couldn't wait till morning?* Then sudden panic caused her body to go numb. She could think of nothing to say.

"Mike was shot by a prowler a little while ago. He was rushed to Floyd Medical Center.

So far, the only report I've received is that he's hanging on, but critical. I'm on my way there now. Hopefully, I will have more information after I get there. I'm sorry I had to be the bearer of such news."

Riley's mind refused to function. She didn't know what to say and simply blurted out, "I'm on my way!"

Later, when she tried to recall this moment in her life, she couldn't remember going to the guest room to alert Trish or to the Edwards' door, but she had done just that. In minutes, the four of them were on their way to Rome. Kirby, having been alerted by Amos, drove his own car, leaving shortly after the others.

They found Chief Nelson with Mr. and Mrs. Unger in the sitting room for emergency services. Davis Morgan was there. Of course, he was. Not because he was police chaplain, but because he cared. It was he who first spoke to Riley. He smiled at her and gripped her right hand with both of his. "He's hanging in there, Riley. The wound is serious, but so far, so good. We've been praying. We know he's in God's hands."

Up to this point Riley had not cried. Perhaps she had been too dazed to do so. But when she approached Mike's parents and saw the sorrowful expressions on their faces, she lost it and began to sob uncontrollably. Trish embraced her, and the two of them wept together. Amos and Carol looked at each other, joined hands and then dropped their heads. It was obvious to all in the room that they were silently praying. A few minutes later Kirby was there. He sat on one side of Riley with Trish on the other as they lovingly watched her, mostly in silence, with an occasional pat on the shoulder or hand. Nathan came with Mike's pastor. Others filtered in throughout the night. It was the longest night Riley had ever experienced.

There was morning light coming in from outside before the doctor in charge of Mike's care entered and summoned the parents along with their pastor to a corner away from others in the room. Riley couldn't hear what the doctor was saying, but she watched the expressions on Mr. and Mrs. Unger's faces closely. Those expressions didn't change. The doctor got up and left the room. The Ungers and the pastor returned to the group. The pastor gave the report. "The doctor told us the bullet went into his ribs just under his right arm, breaking several ribs and doing massive damage. He was taken to surgery for them to remove the slug and make needed repairs. He is presently in surgical recovery.

They will move him to ICU in about an hour. They almost lost him a couple of times during the night. His breathing now seems a little stronger. He's resting in an induced coma, and they are optimistic."

He's still alive, Riley told herself. *That's all that matters now. He's alive.*

***

Charley Nelson was on and off his phone all night. When some of the support group temporarily left to go to the cafeteria for coffee, he motioned for Kirby to come over and sit in a vacated chair beside him. "I thought you might like to know that Jed told us the shooter was driving a white Ford Taurus," Charley said almost before he was seated.

"Then it was probably the kidnapper, Houston," Kirby said, almost spitting out the name.

"Yes, the only thing he took was a rifle."

"Then that's why he was there. He needed a rifle. I'm told he has a handgun. Why did he think he needed a rifle?" Kirby directed the question more to himself than to the chief.

"People like him use rifles for ambush. Please keep a close eye on your sister. That rifle may have been stolen to use against her or Nate."

"I'm going to pass that information on to Amos and several guys who work for us. Having more eyes out there couldn't hurt."

"You do that, but please warn them not to approach the guy. Tell them if they spot anything to call us immediately. I'll also have my men stay close."

"I've got to ask you how this happened. Was Mike not wearing a vest?" Kirby asked.

"He was. It was one of those one-in-a-thousand flukes that no one ever expects to happen. He had his gun raised and pointed toward the burglar, who fired. The shot found the small vulnerable spot under the arm created by Mike raising his arm to aim his gun. If only he had been standing at a different angle, he would have been protected," Charley muttered.

A few minutes later Kirby passed the word on to Amos and asked him to secure the help of the Cleaning Crew to protect Riley. Amos used his phone to immediately make those arrangements. He then found places closer to Riley for him and Carol to sit. For the remainder of the morning, Amos could be seen carefully checking out every person who came into the room.

Kirby left mid-morning, after a brief word and a hug for his sister and a heads up for Amos.

He left Rome and drove straight to the crime scene area. His experience as a detective, as brief as it had been, taught him a lot about the habits of goons like Houston. This thug needed to be put away immediately. People were being hurt and even dying. How hard could it be to find him if he were still in town? Hiding among hundreds of thousands of people can be easy, but it's difficult to disappear in a town of only five thousand. Conventional thinking would be that after shooting a policeman, he would flee the area as quickly as possible. Kirby knew that wasn't likely. Houston was on a mission and his irrational mind would keep him pursuing that objective until it was completed, or he was stopped. Kirby intended to stop him.

He passed the house where he assumed the shooting had occurred—there was an Adairsville police cruiser and another car, probably a GBI vehicle, in the drive. His instincts told him that Houston probably hid somewhere nearby before breaking into the house. As he drove, he looked for any place where one might hide a car for a few hours. About a mile from the scene of the crime, he saw a dilapidated barn sitting off to the right. No fence or any other obstacles to keep a car from being driven into the old barn or perhaps behind it. Kirby parked. He walked to the barn but found no indication that Houston might have been there. He returned to his car and got in to continue his search. Soon he noticed the remnants of a road, probably cut by sawmillers or pulpwooders years earlier.

Kirby pulled onto the little road but decided not to drive his car over it. He got out and started walking. Within five minutes his car was no longer visible, hidden by the trees and bushes. He came to a wide clearing where a car could easily be driven to stay out of sight. He looked around. It took him only a moment to find an empty liquor bottle. He picked it up and took a close look. He continued to walk around the area. There was a bag, like one a convenience store might use for customer purchases, caught low on a tree limb where the wind had undoubtedly propelled it. Kirby felt sure Houston had spent Sunday afternoon here. He guessed he probably would not return to this exact spot. Rather, because of the nearby shooting, he would likely feel more secure going the opposite direction. The area west of town offered a lot of places for him to hide, and that was the area where Nate and the Boyntons lived. That's where he'd be. Kirby was sure of it. He got into his car. Before starting the engine, he called Charley to report his finds and share what he suspected. "Are you still at the hospital?" he asked.

"Still here."

"Any news yet?"

"We haven't heard anything new," the chief told him.

***

Shortly after one o'clock Mike's parents were permitted to go to the ICU to visit with their son, though they were told he would be asleep and unresponsive. A few minutes later, they returned smiling. Mrs. Unger told the group waiting that they were informed the worst of the crisis was over. Barring any complications, Mike would be assigned a patient room later in the day. Tomorrow he would be allowed to awake from the coma and should be somewhat responsive.

Although she still felt a degree of anxiety, Riley felt like a great weight had been lifted. For the first time in the hours since receiving the crushing news, she felt that her mind was properly functioning. She desperately wanted to see Mike, to hold his hand, to kiss his cheek, but she knew that was not possible. Before leaving the hospital, she hugged Mr. and Mrs. Unger and asked them to alert her to any changes in Mike's condition. Her last words to them were, "I won't stop praying."

All through the corridors of the hospital and then in the parking lot, Amos remained no more than an arm's length away from Riley. One would have thought he had received secret service training from the way his eyes constantly moved about to pick up anyone who came close to them. After getting back home, he made sure all doors leading outside were locked. He insisted that Riley and Trish not leave the building without first consulting him.

"You don't have to worry about me leaving. I'm headed for the closest bed," Trish declared as she yawned.

Riley also laid down, but as tired as she was, sleep didn't come easily. Her thoughts were of Mike. *Sweet, gentle, and patient Mike. How could anyone harm him?* She pondered the way Amos hovered over her as they were leaving the hospital and the precautions he took after they got home. Then it came to her. *It was Houston who did this! They are afraid he's coming after me.* She suddenly felt an urge to pray for Nate and Kaylene. *Lord, please put a barrier of safety around those two. Protect them against anything that madman might try to do to them.* She spent the next twenty minutes praying for Mike. Then she was fast asleep.

***

Houston and his rifle were well hidden in a pine thicket just across the road from the old man's mailbox. He had done his homework. He knew that, when home, Bannister always walked from his house to the mailbox to retrieve his mail around two o'clock. He was certain the old man was home because he could see his car. It was a quarter till two. He was glad he had at least ten minutes to rest since he had hidden his car almost two miles away. His walk through the woods to get to this spot left him huffing and puffing. There would be time to catch his breath before he had to make the shot that would net him the money he needed. He lit a cigarette and kept his eyes peeled. Right on schedule, Nate was coming down the long driveway, but he wasn't alone. The Kid was with him, talking and gesturing as she walked beside the old man.

Occasionally she got in front of him, apparently in an effort to make sure he was paying attention to her.

It didn't matter. Maybe he would take her out too. *Two for the price of one.* He quietly laughed at his little joke. Laying on his stomach, he propped himself up on his elbows and prepared to take the shot. He wanted it to be a short shot, a sure thing. They were almost to the box. He carefully aimed. Ready to pull the trigger. Then a car came around the curve and stopped between him and the pair. The driver of the car rolled down his window and chatted with the old man. Houston could hear them talking about cattle. *Come on. Get out of the way.* He waited one minute, then two, until the driver finally drove forward. Houston adjusted his aim as the old man with mail in hand and the girl at his side walked away from him. He pulled the trigger. There was the crack of the rifle firing, but the old man was still standing. He slowly turned in Houston's direction and reached under his shirt. He pulled a gun from under his belt and began to walk slowly toward him with arm raised and gun in hand.

How could he have missed? The stories he had heard were true. *That old man is indestructible!* Houston was overtaken by a surge of panic. He jumped to his feet and ran into the woods. The old man kept walking and then fired once, twice, and a third time. Houston was aware that the third slug had torn into a tree limb not six inches from his head. Carrying his rifle in his right hand, he moved with all the speed his poorly conditioned legs would allow. Then his right foot hit something on the ground, causing him to stumble forward. He dropped his rifle. Quickly jumping to his feet, he grabbed his weapon off the ground to resume his dash through the woods.

Nate stopped in the middle of the road, still holding his gun in his hand. "That ought to let him know I mean business," he muttered, before turning and walking back toward the Kid, who was standing with her mouth wide open. But for once, no words were coming out.

Houston ran without looking back for a good half mile before he collapsed onto the ground, barely able to get his breath. While resting, he kept looking in the direction from which he had come, half expecting to see the old man walking through the woods toward him. *That old man is crazy. Not even bullets can stop him.*

Houston didn't feel safe until he made it back to his car and drove to a spot near the little town of Plainville, a place where he had hidden earlier. He sat there catching his breath, trying to decide what to do next.

***

After getting the good news from Amos about Mike's condition, Kirby decided to keep his afternoon appointment with Randy Tate, Nate's opposition in the special election for county commissioner. He would be looking for anything that might indicate he was Houston's boss, or anything that might eliminate him. They met at Tate's insurance office in Cartersville. "Thank you for seeing me," Kirby said when the secretary escorted him into the office of the middle-aged candidate. "I'll not take a lot of your time. Due to my uncle's generosity, my sister and I have a number of businesses and properties in Bartow County. So, you can understand why I have a genuine interest in the commissioner's race. It's important to us that the right man be in that office, but we're not sure who the right man is. I just wanted to get to know you and maybe ask a few questions."

"I'm more than happy to have you come by. I'm aware of your business interests and have wanted to meet you," Tate told him.

"Maybe you could give me a little background information," Kirby suggested.

"There's not a lot to tell. I grew up in middle Georgia where my dad had an insurance business much like this one. While I was at the University of Georgia, he pulled up roots and moved everything here. He felt that, from a business perspective, this was the better place to be. After graduation I came here and went to work for him. I met my wife in Cartersville. We've been married for thirty-one years and have a son and a daughter. We lost a son to leukemia a few years back. When Dad retired, I took over the business. It hasn't made me rich, but it's been good to me."

"I understand you've held a couple of other elected positions with the county. Could you tell me about that?" Kirby asked.

"Back when our children were younger, I spent one four-year term as a member of the school board. I chose to not run again because I saw an opportunity to become tax commissioner. I served one term in that position, but the next time around, the citizens elected another man. I wasn't too disappointed when that happened."

"And why was that?" Kirby asked.

"No particular reason. It just wasn't my cup of tea."

"Why do you want to be county commissioner?"

"That's always been my goal. It's the position I've wanted all along. It offers opportunity to step in and help this county become the dynamic place I know it can be."

"And why do you feel you're a better choice than Nate Bannister?" Kirby asked.

"Well, I have more experience than he does. He's popular with a lot of our people because he was a ballplayer. A good one, I understand. But he has nothing in his background that indicates he would be a good county commissioner. I'm much more progressive than he is. I'm afraid he would hold us back rather than help us move forward. And to be frank, Mr. Gordan, he scares me just a little."

"Why do you say that?"

"From what I understand, he's always been pretty independent, set on doing things his own way. You just never know what he's going to do next."

"I understand," Kirby said. "Do you have any personal history with the man?"

"I hardly know him," Tate answered. "No real history. I just know what my research about him tells me. It seems to me he is rather unreliable."

The two men talked for a few more minutes before Kirby shook Tate's hand and departed.

Upon getting home, Kirby received the disturbing news from Amos that someone had taken a shot at Nate and Kaylene, but both were unscathed. *He's got to be stopped and stopped soon,* Kirby told himself.

CHAPTER 16

Riley flashed a subdued smile in Trish's direction as she returned to the hospital lobby from her visit to Mike's room. "How is he?" Trish asked as they walked toward the parking lot.

"As expected, he is conscious, but groggy. He tried to keep a stiff upper lip, but, obviously, he is having some pain. The good news is that the real danger is over. Recovery will take a while but, praise be to God, his life is no longer in jeopardy." Riley's voice broke a bit as she spoke. Trish put her arm around Riley's shoulder and pulled her close.

They were silent during most of the drive back to Adairsville. Riley appreciated that Trish respected her need to be alone with her thoughts.

Shortly after entering the Adairsville city limits, Riley's thoughts were interrupted when she was startled by a cry from Trish. "Look out, Riley!" At that moment, she became vaguely aware of someone on the highway directly in front of her. She swerved sharply to her left in an effort to avoid a collision with the staggering figure. Fortunately, there was no westbound traffic at that moment, allowing her to safely bring her car to a stop on the opposite side of the road. She panicked for a moment, not sure if she missed or hit the person now lying on the highway. Both ladies quickly sprang out of the car. Riley ran toward the heap lying in the road. Trish instinctively took a position to stop or redirect any oncoming traffic.

Riley fell to her knees and lifted the head and upper body of the man in the road. She immediately caught a whiff. that took her back to her days of service at the Boston Mission. This man was, no doubt, thoroughly intoxicated. "Are you alright?" she asked. He opened his dark, sad eyes and looked into her face before grunting something unintelligible. Again, Riley asked, "Are you alright?"

This time she heard a raspy voice reply with slurred words, "Yeah. I'm alright." The fallen man was now trying to lift himself off the pavement but wasn't having much luck. He finally turned and got on his knees. Riley was now sure he had not been hit by her car. His impairment was alcohol related.

"We've got to get you off this road," Riley told him, taking hold of one of his arms and pulling upward. He got one foot on the ground and then the other. Riley put one of his arms around her shoulder and took as much of his weight as possible. They slowly moved toward the grass beside the road. Riley helped him to ease to the ground. It was then that she recognized him. This drunken and broken piece of humanity collapsed on the ground at her feet was Ole Buster, the man whose story Mike had shared with her a few days earlier. Instantly her attitude was transformed from disgust to pity. *It's funny how our feelings can so abruptly change about a person when we know his story*, she reasoned.

With Riley and Buster now off the road, Trish abandoned her post as traffic director and hurried over to where the two had safely located. "What's wrong with him? Is he alright?" Trish asked.

"Just about everything you can imagine is wrong with him," Riley replied. "This is Buster. Remember? Mike told us about Buster."

"Oh yes. I remember," Trish responded in a tone that revealed her grasp of the situation. "So he is, ah . . ."

"You've got it," Riley quickly shot back. "He's 'three sheets to the wind' as they used to say down at the mission."

"What are we going to do, Riley? We can't leave him sitting here on the side of the road!"

Buster turned his head toward Trish's raised voice. Instantly his mouth dropped open, and a strange sound came from his mouth. He lifted his right arm and pointed a finger in Trish's direction. "Lois," he shouted in a clear voice that gave no hint of his condition. "Lois," he cried again, this time with both arms stretched out toward the stunned Trish. Then his body fell limp and sprawled on the ground.

"Is he dead?" Trish asked with panic in her voice.

"No," Riley answered. "He's passed out. Maybe I need to call Amos. He'll know what we need to do." She reached for her phone.

After Riley explained what had happened and where they were and assured Amos that she and Trish had no injuries, he told her that he and Bill would be there in five minutes.

As Riley put her phone away, Trish asked, "Did Buster call me Lois?"

"I think he did. Didn't Mike say his deceased wife's name was Lois? I think there is something about you that reminded him of her. Maybe you resemble her. Maybe it's your voice."

"That's a little eerie," Trish said. "But it's also sweet. To think, I remind him of the lost love that put him on this track," she said pointing toward the slumbering body on the ground.

"Just remember, he's dead drunk, and probably won't remember anything about what happened here tomorrow."

"I guess so," Trish said, sounding a little sad.

A few minutes later Amos and Bill arrived in the Cleaning Crew van. "Are you girls sure you're not hurt?" Amos anxiously asked when he exited the passenger side.

"We're fine," Riley responded. "Just a little shaken and confused about what to do with our friend here." She pointed toward Buster, who was now on his side making a sound that sounded something like snoring.

"The only thing I know to do is to load him in the van and deliver him to Charley. He can sleep it off in the holding cell, get some food in his stomach, and then start the whole process over again."

"I don't know, Amos. Isn't there something we can do to help him?" Riley asked with a note of frustration in her voice.

"I don't know what it would be. People have been trying to help Buster for years, but he has refused everything anybody has tried to do. Carol and I tried to talk with him and offered to help him get medical help, but he wants no part of it."

"Let me take him home with me," Bill, who had remained silent up until this moment, said. "I would like to have a shot at helping him get on his feet. The guys and I have noticed him around town, and we feel like we might be able to make a difference. A couple of us have been there, you know."

"Sounds like a plan to me. You would know what you are getting into," Amos said. "More power to you. Let's load him in the van, and we will turn him over to you."

"You're so sweet to do this," Riley said, placing her right hand on Bill's shoulder. "You don't know how proud I am of you and the guys."

"We're just trying to pay back the debt we owe for what you, Kirby, and Amos have done for us. I think they call it payin' forward. We'll do our best to help this man like you have helped us."

"I'll be praying for you, and if there is any way I can help you with this, just let me know," Riley told him. She couldn't wait to get home and tell Kirby about this latest development. It was another positive step in what she considered their most important project.

***

Kirby's mind was active as he drove south on Highway 41. Riley had brought two pieces of information that pleased him beyond words. She reported that Mike was off the critical list. Yes, he had a long recovery ahead of him, but all things remaining equal, he would make it with no lingering effects. Kirby was not as close to Mike as Riley, but he thought highly of the young policeman and considered him a good friend. He had been thanking God repeatedly since receiving that news.

Riley's second news bulletin had been a delightful surprise. Bill had volunteered to aid the old derelict called Buster. He had often seen Buster staggering around town but did not know his story until Riley shared some of it with him. Being one who had paid his dues as a street cop in a medium-sized city, Kirby often had contact with such people. He understood that some of their stories were contrived for the purpose of getting another bottle of booze, but he also knew many of them had indeed allowed difficult circumstances to get the best of them. Helping such people was difficult at best. He was proud of Bill for stepping up to attempt to make a difference in Buster's life. He hoped Bill and his compatriots would not find the task too daunting and allow discouragement to halt their own progress. The Cleaning Crew was an experiment in salvaging lives that seemed to be going well, but he appreciated how fragile the plan was. Yes, he was proud of the guys, but he would be praying that this endeavor did not cause a setback.

Then there was this business with Houston and whoever was behind his escapades. Naturally, he feared for his sister's life. To protect her, he must discover the driving force behind all the trouble. He needed more to go on. That was why he was on his way to meet with Jason Purcell, the character from the Outdoor Sportsman.

After a couple of minutes, Kirby spotted the restaurant on the right. When the appointment was made, Purcell suggested they meet there for a cup of coffee. Kirby wasn't much of a coffee drinker, but he was glad to oblige the company representative for the opportunity to have a conversation with him. It didn't seem likely to him that someone in Purcell's position with such an up-and-coming company would be guilty of such devious behavior, but he certainly needed to be checked out.

When Kirby walked into the barely occupied establishment, he looked around for someone fitting the description he had been given of Purcell. Just then, a slim, nicely dressed man of perhaps forty years of age got up from the table where he was sitting with a slightly older guy. He smiled and walked in Kirby's direction. "Are you Kirby Gordan?" The gentleman extended a hand toward him.

"Yes, I'm Kirby, and I assume you are Jason Purcell." Kirby shook his hand and made eye contact while speaking.

"I hope you don't mind that I brought along Kenneth Cotes, who will probably be our general contractor when we start breaking ground in your little town."

"That's fine," Kirby answered. "I want to get as much information as possible. Perhaps he will be able to answer some of my questions." *Kenneth Cotes. I know that name.* Then it came to him. *Kenneth Cotes is the man who accused Nate of killing his dog. It didn't get any better than this. He had two of the possible suspects at his disposal.*

Kirby greeted Cotes. The waitress came over when he was seated. "I assume you are joining these two gentlemen for coffee. Is there anything else I can get you?" she asked.

"No, coffee will be great," Kirby said. He then turned to Purcell. "Why don't you tell me about your proposed project."

"Thrilled to do that." Purcell laid out his sales pitch in pretty much the same way Kirby had heard it from Riley and Amos. "I'm delighted to have Kenneth in on the project." He motioned toward Cotes. "I'm learning how hard it is to find good help."

"Tell me about yourself, Jason. Will you be moving on after doing the groundwork here?" Kirby asked.

"No, actually, if we are able to pull it all together, I will remain to run our operation here. It will be a dream come true for me. I started at the bottom fifteen years ago as a clerk at one of our stores. The rise up the ladder has been gradual. My preliminary assignment here is a kind of test for me. They tell me if I can make it happen, it will be mine. And you know it's not like managing a small retail store. Outdoor Sportsman isn't only a store, it's an experience. It'll draw thousands to your town monthly."

"And what if plans don't come together here? What'll you do then? Will you be given another assignment with the company?" Kirby asked.

"I don't know," Purcell answered. "I may not have a job, or I may find myself back in one of the stores working as a clerk again."

"So, this is extremely important to you," Kirby stated. "I guess you'd do just about anything to make it happen."

"Just about," Purcell responded.

"And what about you, Kenneth?" Kirby asked the other man who so far had remained almost silent. "How important is it to you?"

"Well, it's not a do or die for us," Cotes replied. "But it would be one of our bigger jobs. We see it as a real opportunity."

"I understand the deal's off if Nate Bannister is elected county commissioner," Kirby said glancing toward Purcell.

"That's right. The company knows that Bannister is against the project. If he is elected, eventually it would need his stamp of approval. The powers that be have no desire to be involved in such a fight. So, if he is elected, the project will be scrapped automatically."

"Which leaves you out in the cold."

"Pretty much so," the ambitious representative admitted.

"And what about you, how do you feel about Nate Bannister?" Kirby asked, looking toward Kenneth Cotes.

"I just don't like the man," he said. "We have had run-ins in the past. I would rather just about anyone be county commissioner other than him. The possibility of losing this job is just one more reason for me to do whatever I can do to keep that old devil out of office."

"Did you gentlemen know that someone took a shot at Nate recently?" Kirby asked, watching the men across the table for their reactions.

Cotes looked surprised, but Kirby wondered how much of it was acting. Purcell, with a blank look on his face said, "You don't say. I don't want him to be commissioner, but I don't want him dead. Who would do something like that?"

"My time as a policeman convinced me there are a lot of violent people out there. You never know," Kirby said, first looking into Purcell's face and then into the eyes of Cotes.

They talked about the project for another ten minutes. "I don't like to make swift decisions. I'll ponder all this and talk with my decision-making team. We'll get back to you," Kirby told Purcell as he got up from the table. "It was good to meet both of you gentlemen."

Driving back toward Adairsville, Kirby reflected on his conversation with the two men. He had learned little he didn't already know about Kenneth Cotes, but he had discovered that Purcell might have a stronger motive than what he had anticipated. *Still no clear-cut suspect,* he decided.

***

Carol came into the living room after finishing the evening dishes to find Amos stretched out in his recliner napping. "You're not going to sleep a wink tonight if you don't liven up a little. Sit up and talk with me. I haven't had anyone to talk with all day."

Amos rubbed his eyes and reached down for the lever to his right, pushing on it to enable his chair to move one notch closer to sitting position. "What do you want to talk about? I sure wouldn't want you to go through a day without conversation," he remarked teasingly.

"I don't know!" his wife of almost forty-five years countered. "How do you feel about Bill taking in Buster? Do you think he can do him any good?"

"I think Bill's heart is in the right place, but I wonder if Buster has reached the point where he is beyond help. I guess he has sunk about as low as a person can go."

"No one is beyond help. As long as there is life, there is hope. Our God is a miracle worker."

"I know he is," Amos replied. "And I think that is what it's going to take. It will take a miracle for Buster to ever walk straight again."

"But wouldn't it be wonderful if Buster, after all these years, could kick the booze habit and get his life back together? Maybe get a job and start living a useful life? That would be a real testimony to what God can do, wouldn't it?"

"Like old Stuart Hamblen's song says, 'It is no secret what God can do,'" Amos replied with a yawn.

"Well, that's what I'm going to be praying for," Carol declared. "I'm going to be praying that God will work a miracle and get Buster back on his feet."

"You do that, Honey, and while you're praying for Buster don't forget to offer up petitions for Mike, and for Riley's safety. You might want to pray that the Lord will help Kirby find out who's behind all the foolishness and put a stop to it."

"I've not stopped asking God's help in any of those matters." There were a few moments of silence before Carol continued. "Do you remember when life was nice and calm around here, without all the drama?"

"Life has always been an adventure with you, old woman," Amos said before closing his eyes and again laying his head back on his chair.

CHAPTER 17

Amos met the Cleaning Crew at the Little Rock. It was their custom to have breakfast together either there or at Crackle Barrel a couple of mornings a week. Amos had already secured a table when Bill and Juan came into the crowded little restaurant.

"Where's Jessie?" Amos inquired after his initial greeting. "I've never known him to miss a meal."

"You're right, the man likes to eat," Bill answered. "This morning is his scheduled time to stay with Buster. One of us needs to be with him all the time. The ladies can't handle him."

Before Bill finished his statement, Kirby came through the door. "I hope you guys don't mind me joining you. I woke up hungry this morning and decided a good solution to that problem would be breakfast at the Little Rock."

"Thrilled to have you," Amos responded. "Jessie is with Buster this morning."

"How's that project going?" Kirby asked, turning toward Bill.

"Well, I'll just say, he still has a long way to go, but we didn't expect it to be easy," Bill said. "He's been on the juice for a long time, and we're not goin' to get him off it overnight. We knew that goin' in. He constantly yells for someone to bring him a drink and when we don't, he tries to get up and go get it himself. It's almost like he can't face life without booze to soften the blow."

"The man has been through a lot, losing his family in a terrible accident," Amos said, looking down at the table.

"He keeps crying out for Lois. I assume that was his wife," Juan said.

"Yeah, Lois was his wife, a beautiful girl from a loving, hard-working family. I was proud of Buster and Lois. It was obvious they loved one another. They were a beautiful little family, makin' a fine life for themselves when the accident occurred. Years have passed, but obviously Buster still hasn't even started to deal with it," Amos reflected.

"He keeps saying somethin' about seein' Lois. Do you think he's hallucinating?" Bill asked.

"Riley's friend, Trish, resembles Lois. In his drunken state the other night when Riley almost hit him, he imagined that Trish was Lois." Amos was then silent for a moment as if in deep thought before going on. "Maybe we need to arrange for Riley and Trish to pay Buster a visit. Perhaps they can offer him some motivation."

"Sounds like a solid idea to me. We'll see if we can make that happen soon," Kirby told them. "I feel sure Riley will be receptive to the idea, and I can't imagine Trish not cooperating. It certainly can't make things worse than they are presently. I appreciate what you guys are trying to do for Buster. You know it's a longshot, don't you?"

"We know, Kirby," Bill responded. "But I also know that we lose nothin' by tryin', and, who knows, we might do some good."

"Amen," Amos said in a voice loud enough to cause the people at the closest table to look in their direction.

When Nate Bannister entered the café with Sam Boynton at his side, all the chatter stopped. Almost everyone looked in the direction of the two men for a few seconds before getting back to their conversation and food. "You would think with a madman gunning for him, Nate would be more careful about walking into crowds like this one," Kirby said.

"You can't scare old Nate. And besides, he's politicking. One can't win an election from an easy chair," Amos declared. "I'm more concerned about him and Mayor Ellison, over there, being in the same room." Amos turned his head toward a corner where the mayor was at a table holding court with two of his constituents.

"Why do you say that? Is there bad blood between Nate and the Mayor?" Kirby asked.

"I don't know if I would call it *bad blood*, but there are definitely some crucial political differences between the two. The mayor has been extremely vocal about some of those issues, and Nate doesn't take criticism well. There is potential for a battle royale any time the two are in the same room."

That's interesting, Kirby thought, mentally adding the mayor to the bottom of his suspect list. He was glad that no ruckus erupted between the two older fireballs before he and his three companions left, their stomachs full and ready to face the day. On the way out they stopped to greet Nate and Sam.

***

The boss knew something had to be done about Houston. He was a loose cannon that could bring him down. He pulled his vehicle into the parking lot of the Oothcaloga Baptist Church and drove around the west side of the building to the back of the graveyard. There he and his vehicle were shielded from the main road by the rise that highlighted numerous head stones. He stopped the car and killed the engine to wait for his rogue hireling.

The late afternoon sun was shining bright. He wished it was dark, because darkness was best for a meeting like this one. He waited about ten more minutes before he saw a car approaching. He assumed it was Houston's current transportation coming toward him. The white Ford stopped just behind him. He stalled long enough for the driver to get out of the car before he put on his baseball cap and sunglasses. He opened his own car door to step out.

"We can talk in my car," Houston suggested.

"No, I'd rather stretch my legs. We can talk here."

"Whatever you say. Like I told you on the phone, I've given it my best shot, but that old man just won't go down. It's getting too hot for me, and I've got to get away from here. I know I haven't completed the contract, but I've got to have some cash. I don't necessarily have to have the full amount, but I need at least half the payoff we talked about."

"Why should I give you anything? Not only have you failed in your mission, but you've messed things up royally. The old fool is sure to be elected, thanks to you. No, I'll not give you a cent."

"You'd better think twice about that. If you don't come through with some dough, everyone in this county is goin' to know you've been behind all the bad things that have been goin' on in this town. When they find out you're the one responsible for that little girl's problems and the attempt on that old ballplayer's life, they'll probably be ready to lynch you."

"You can't tell anyone without incriminating yourself. There's no way you'll go to the law without putting your own neck in a noose."

"Don't you believe it! I've got it all figured out. If you ignore my request, you're a goner, partner. You can depend on that."

"That's blackmail. You can't do that!"

"You can call it whatever you want, but that's the way it is. You'd better let that sink in if you value your freedom."

The man who had prided himself with being in control of every situation now lowered his head. After a moment he reluctantly mumbled, "Okay, you've got me over a barrel. There's nothing else I can do. I don't have the money on me. I'll have to get it in the morning. I'll meet you here at ten o'clock."

"Now you're talking," Houston responded. "I knew you would see it my way when you knew all the facts. I'll see you at ten in the morning." He turned to walk toward his car.

The other man reached into his pocket and pulled out a small handgun. He pointed it toward Houston's back and pulled the trigger three times. Houston fell to the ground, facedown.

The shooter remained in the same position for an instant, the gun still raised. *I didn't know if I could do it. But it was easy. I feel no different than I would if it had been a mad dog. He's dead and I'm glad.*

He left the body lying in the position in which it had fallen. He got into his car and drove away.

***

The ten-year old boy loved to slip away from his grandparents' house on the hill and play Robin Hood in the woods behind the old cemetery. He especially liked to climb the big oak tree, where he could keep watch for the Sheriff of Nottingham and his men. Now on a branch two-thirds of the way up the tree, he almost allowed a cry of horror to escape his mouth before catching and stifling it. *That man just shot the other! I don't believe it. I just saw a man shoot someone!* He was some distance away. It was difficult to see through the tops of the trees between him and the cemetery, but he could see well enough to know what just took place. He watched the man wearing the green baseball cap and sunglasses stand there for at least a full minute after shooting, holding the gun in his hand. The man then opened the car door, got in, and drove away.

The boy didn't move until the car was out of sight. He quickly made his way down the tree with less care than he would normally take for the descent, causing him to almost fall before catching hold of a firm branch. His feet hit the ground running and sustained their speed until he covered the half mile back to his grandparents' house. Now out of breath, he entered through the back door. *Should I tell anyone? I'll have to think about it.* He sat down in front of the TV to watch a rerun of an episode of the old Robin Hood series. But his mind could not erase what he had just seen in the graveyard. Sooner or later, he would have to tell someone, but right now he didn't want to talk about it.

***

Jimmy was now retired from the manufacturing company for which he had labored for almost forty years. For nine years before retirement, he had hurried home after work and given up many of his Saturdays to do lawn care for neighbors and small businesses. Now that he was free from the factory, he continued to keep up yards. The business had grown to the extent that he could no longer handle it alone. He was lucky to have Larry as his right-hand man. Larry, the son of a friend, was a dependable worker. This was the second season that they had worked together, and Jimmy hoped their association would last for a long time.

One of their biggest jobs was keeping up the Oothcaloga church cemetery, and today was the day. Hoping to get ahead of the heat, they arrived at the cemetery before eight o'clock. As they unloaded their equipment on the west side of the church parking lot, Jimmy noticed the backside of a car on the far side of the hill. "There's someone parked back there. Let's not disturb them," he told Larry. Jimmy mowed on the front side of the hill while Larry used the trimmer around the graves. By nine-thirty Jimmy had mowed his way to the top of the hill. The car was still there. He began to suspect that something might be off kilter. He got off his mower and walked to a spot where he could observe the north side of the burial ground. It was then that he saw someone lying face down next to a grave. Jimmy shouted Larry's name twice before the young man heard him and shut off the trimmer. "Someone is hurt down there. Call 911!" he yelled as he ran down the hill toward the still body. A clumsy attempt to find a pulse produced nothing. Soon an emergency unit and a police car were on the scene, and the investigation was underway.

***

It was two days after the town began to talk about a dead man being found in the Oothcaloga cemetery that Kirby came to Chief Nelson's office for a fact-finding visit.

"I suppose, since you are sometimes a consultant to this department, and this case might be pertinent to your family, we can talk about it."

"What do you mean, 'pertinent to my family?'" Kirby asked.

"I mean the Kid has identified the man we found dead in Oothcaloga cemetery as Houston, the scum who kidnapped her, the one who threatened your sister, and possibly the lowlife who shot Mike. The rifle that was stolen that night was found in the car parked in the cemetery."

"Wow, you can't imagine how that eases my mind," Kirby told the chief. "I don't like to hear that anyone has died, but I am elated to hear the threat to Riley has run its course. Do you have any idea who killed him?"

"At this moment, not a clue. However, we do have an eyewitness."

"Well, that ought to help. Who is your witness?"

"Of course, I can't tell you his name, but he's a ten-year-old boy who happened to be playing in the woods behind the cemetery at the time. He saw everything that happened from his perch high in an oak tree. He didn't know the man who did the shooting. About all he had to tell us was that the man wore a green baseball-type cap, a light green shirt, and sunglasses. All he could tell us about the car the shooter drove was that it was white. And, oh, the shooter held the small gun in his right hand. He shot the victim in the back three times and stayed frozen, in shooting position, for a few moments before turning around and getting into his car. He didn't even walk over to examine his handiwork."

"Sounds like a pretty cold character," Kirby remarked. "Do you think the shooter might be the man who hired Houston to get Nate out of the election?"

"Regardless of what I told you, it would be only a guess. Who knows? The boss may have felt his identity was in danger of being revealed by Houston's sloppiness."

"Obviously, I'm thrilled that Riley is no longer in danger from that madman," Kirby remarked. "But I've got a feeling the danger may still be real for Nate. He remains a candidate, and we both know that a man like Houston could care less about who is Bartow County commissioner. If it was the boss who killed Houston, he may now be ready to take care of Nate himself."

Kirby decided, after leaving the police department, that the first thing he needed to do was to see if the account of the shooter being right-handed eliminated anyone on his suspect list. He wished the shooter had been left-handed, but perhaps that would make it too easy.

He knew from having coffee with them that Purcell and Cotes were right-handed. They remained on his list. He used his desktop to find pictures of both Mayor Ellison and commissioner candidate Randy Tate signing documents with their right hands. Couldn't eliminate them either. Now he needed to find out about Edward Neff, the storekeeper who had kept a running feud with Nate going for years. That should be easy enough. Kirby went by Neff's convenience store, put several items on the counter and watched Mr. Neff ring them up with his left hand. Being left-handed, he was removed from Kirby's suspect list. He could not have been the killer. Now there were four, but perhaps the guilty man was not even on his list. None of them seemed to rise to the top. He wished he could talk with the boy who had witnessed the killing in the cemetery, but he respected Charley's decision to keep his identity concealed. It was the right thing to do, and Charley Nelson was a man who seemed always to favor doing the right thing. *Oh well.* Now that Riley was apparently out of danger, it was no longer his problem. Charley could handle it. Since Riley no longer needed a bodyguard, he felt free to see if he could get tickets for that show Connie wanted to see at the Fox in Atlanta. But no matter how hard he tried, he couldn't delete the mystery from his mind. He knew he could have no peace of mind until the culprit was behind bars.

CHAPTER 18

Trish was uncharacteristically quiet as they headed toward the apartment where Bill and his wife lived. "What's on your mind, Trish?" Riley asked.

"What makes you think there's something on my mind?" Trish snapped back. "You may not know me as well as you think you do."

"I know you well enough to know that when you're not saying much and you get that look on your face, you're usually concerned about something."

"What look? My face is the same as always. There's no look on my face."

"I'm talking about that blank stare that causes you to appear to be straining to see something far away."

Trish flipped the sun visor down and glared into the mirror. "I don't look like that!"

"Not now. Now you just look mad."

"I'm sorry Riley. I didn't mean to be an old grump. It's just that I'm a little uptight about talking with Buster. The guys keep telling me he has been asking for the girl that looks like Lois. So I look like his deceased wife. That doesn't mean I've got magic words that will take away all his troubles. What can I say to him?"

"I think Bill and the fellows think he might be inclined to listen to what you have to say. They are looking for something that will motivate him to at least exert a little effort to dry out. Just firmly, but gently speak to him as you would to anyone else in that situation."

"That's the problem. I don't know what I would say to anyone."

"It'll come to you. I'll be right there at your side. I've been praying all morning, and I know there's a third person who'll be there to pick up the slack. As Christians, we always have a power beyond ourselves. We never have to depend on our own cleverness."

"Boy, I'm glad for that. I'd never get anything done if I had to count on my own shrewdness," Trish laughed.

"You're as sharp as anyone I know, but all of us need the Lord's help. It's just a fact of life," Riley assured her as she guided the car into a parking spot in front of Bill and Judy's apartment.

"Well, here we are. I guess it's now or never." Trish took a deep breath and stepped out of the car.

After a brief exchange with Bill and Judy, Judy ushered them into the room where Buster was stretched out on the bed in a plaid shirt and baggy jeans. His eyes were wide open and staring at the ceiling. Riley had seen some sad cases during the months she volunteered at the mission in Boston, but she didn't think she had ever laid eyes on anyone who looked more pathetic than Buster at this moment. The hardness and unnatural configuration of his bearded face immediately told her this was a truly tortured human being. Jessie was sitting in a chair beside the bed—a seat that evidently one or other of the three members of the Cleaning Crew had occupied relentlessly now for several days.

"Look Buster, you've got company. It's Miss Riley and the lady you've been asking for," Jessie announced. He stood to his feet and motioned for Trish to take the seat beside the bed.

Trish hesitated and turned to look at Riley, who nodded and turned her eyes toward the empty chair. Trish, a bit reluctantly, moved forward and flopped into the chair. "Hi Buster. We thought you might like to see somebody other than these guys," she said glancing toward Jessie. "I know they've been taking good care of you, but it's always good to have new friends drop by."

Buster said nothing but turned his head to focus on Trish. For a moment he stared, and then his face made the most drastic transformation. Suddenly his expression was one that might have suggested adoration—even joy. Riley had never seen a face change so completely, so suddenly. He continued to stare at the girl in the chair. She was obviously aware, maybe even touched, by the man's response to her, for she seemed to be speechless. Finally, she spoke. "We hear you've been having a hard time."

"I know you can't be her, but you look exactly like her." Buster's low volume and slurred speech made it difficult for the others in the room to understand, but Trish comprehended every word.

"I look like who?" Trish asked.

"You remind me of Lois, my wife," Buster said. "You could be her twin. She died, you know. Terrible accident, but you look just like her."

"Tell me about the accident?" Trish requested. Riley was impressed by Trish's quick wit. She knew that to deal with a tragedy, one usually needed to talk about it.

"I don't like to think about it," Buster blurted out. "Will you hold my hand?" He made his appeal in a matter-of-fact manner.

Trish was a little taken aback by the request. "I'll hold your hand if you'll tell me about the accident." She took hold of his left hand that was resting on the bed. "I know it's hard, but you can do it. Just tell me what you remember about the accident. How long since it happened?"

"I don't know. Maybe a couple of years ago. Maybe it's been longer. I don't know. I can't remember."

"What do you remember about it?" Trish asked.

"I know it was the worst day of my life," he said, not taking his eyes off her. "I lost my beautiful wife, my boy, and my two little girls. I lost everything that day."

"Yes, you lost more than anyone should have to lose all at once, but you didn't lose everything."

"I lost everything," he repeated. "And it was my fault."

"It wasn't your fault," Trish responded firmly. "It was an accident."

"I should have taken time off and driven them to the doctor. It was my fault, and nothin' will change that. Had to make that dollar. Couldn't do what Lois asked me to do. She was up all night with the baby, but I insisted on goin' to work. I killed them! I have nothin' left."

"You still have your life, but if you keep on drinking, you'll not have that very much longer."

"Yes, it'll be over then. I'll be glad when that time comes."

"There're a lot of us who would be sad if that should happen, those of us who are your friends."

"I don't have any friends. Who's going to be sad if I die today?"

"I'm your friend, and Riley is your friend. All these guys who are taking care of you are your friends. They all want you to get well and make the most of the life you have. Don't you think that is what Lois would want? She wouldn't want you to throw away your life, would she? She loved you and would want you to do the best you can without her. These guys are trying to help you get back on your feet. They want you to again be the person Lois would be proud of." Trish turned her head toward Jessie. "Will you work with these guys? Will you do that for Lois? I know that's what she would want you to do, and it's what I want you to do. Will you do that?"

There was a long silence before Buster replied. "For Lois, I'll try," he said.

"Will you promise me that you will try your best? These guys are doing everything they can to help you. Will you promise me you will buckle down and do what they tell you to do?"

"For Lois, I'll try," Buster repeated. Riley thought she saw a faint smile on his face, but maybe it was her imagination.

Before leaving Buster's room, Riley did something she had learned from Amos and Carol. They never left a trying situation without talking with the Lord about it. "Buster, before we leave, we want to pray with you." Riley bowed her head and the others in the room followed suit. She began to pray: "Lord, you know Buster has had a hard time. Help him to know that he is not alone. May he realize that we are with him and want to help him, but, most of all, help him to know that you desire to step into his life and make a difference."

After finishing her prayer, Riley saw Trish lean over and touch Buster's shoulder. "We'll be back to see you soon," she promised.

When they were outside the apartment, Riley turned and embraced her friend. "Trish, you're amazing. You handled that beautifully. I'm so proud of you."

"You were right. I wasn't on my own. I felt the Spirit leading me. I just hope we did some good. My heart breaks for that man. He not only suffered a brutal loss, but evidently, he has been carrying the guilt for ten years," Trish remarked.

"And probably this was the first time he's spoken about it. You're going to have to stay around a while longer. We'll plan to visit with him every day or two for a while," Riley announced. She was glad for a logical reason to keep Trish with her. She was growing accustomed to having her closest friend at her side.

They got into Riley's car and headed toward Calhoun to visit with Mike on his first full day home from the hospital. *It's a good day*, Riley decided. She began to hum a little chorus she had grown to love. Soon both she and Trish were singing the words together.

***

Nate was surprised when Charley Nelson and a GBI agent showed up at his home to question him about the shooting of some man by the name of Houston. According to them, he was the one who had kidnapped the Kid. He was also probably the one who had taken a shot at him out by the mailbox. He assured them he knew nothing of the man or the shooting, and they seemed to be satisfied with his alibi.

He knew the dead man was nothing more than a patsy for someone who wanted him out of the way. He wasn't ready to let that go yet. He was keeping close tabs on the Kid. In his mind, Kenneth Cotes, his long-time nemesis, was the likely perpetrator, but as of yet, he had no proof.

Today Nate was at a downtown Cartersville radio station where he was scheduled for an interview. He had learned after accepting the question-and-answer session that the station was partly owned by Cotes. He was greeted by a receptionist who led him to a lounge area that reminded him of a hospital waiting room. He was seated there alone. Station programming came to him loud and clear from a speaker on the wall. Being a former ballplayer who was often in the spotlight, he had done numerous interviews. He never had a problem doing those, but these political interrogations put him a little on edge. A middle-aged man with long hair came into the room and introduced himself as Roy Wright, the interviewer. Roy took him into the studio and showed him where to sit. A couple of minutes later, they were on the air.

There was a brief introduction, then, quicker than one of Nate's fastballs in his prime, the first question was thrown at him. "Nate, no one questions your greatness as a baseball player, but what qualifications do you have for serving as county commissioner?" Roy asked.

"I don't believe that having a background in politics is crucial to being a good commissioner. The most fundamental qualification is common sense, and I believe that is something I have. Also, Bartow County has always been my home. Even when I was playing baseball, I spent the off-season right here in this county. The commissioner needs to be someone who loves this place and will stand ready to protect it and promote it. Anyone who knows me will tell you I'm that kind of person."

"You do have your critics, Nate," Roy interjected.

"Yes, I do. I suppose anyone who runs for office will face some opposition. I haven't heard of anyone lately winning an election unanimously. If you had listened closely to my statement a moment ago, you would have noticed I said, '*Anyone who knows me* will tell you I am that kind of person.' Obviously, not everyone knows me. That's why I agree to do interviews like this one."

"I've heard it said that we would be better off with a younger man in that office. How do you feel about that?"

"There's something to be said for youth and new ideas, but the wisdom of age is also beneficial. I might also point out that my opponent is no spring chicken either," Nate added.

"Actually, you've got around twenty years on him," Wright informed him.

"Is that right? I would have guessed our ages were a lot closer. I suspect my fastball is still harder than his, and I wouldn't be surprised if my time around the bases isn't a few seconds faster than his," Nate laughed.

"I don't know about that," Roy said, at a loss to come up with a clever response. He cleared his throat before proceeding. "I've been informed that you were recently questioned by the authorities concerning an incident in Adairsville? Can you tell us about that?"

"I thought we were here to discuss the commissioner's office and the coming election," Nate told him. There was a moment of silence before Nate went on. "I suppose there is no harm in offering an explanation. I would not want anyone to be misled. Yes, I understand that a man was shot to death in our little town recently. Our police chief and a GBI agent came to talk with me because they concluded that the victim had harmed a friend of mine and may have taken a shot at me a few days ago. I assured them I knew nothing about the man or his death. They told me the approximate time of his demise, and I provided details to them of where I was at the time. That pleased them. We were good friends when they left my house. We have a dandy police chief in Adairsville, and I'm sure he has things under control. Don't doubt for a moment that he'll get his man."

Nate now had no doubt he had been set up. He was tempted to walk out of the interview. Perhaps it was the competitive spirit of the old ballplayer that kept him there until the program came to an end. The questions were more of the same, designed to put him on the spot. However, the he kept his composure and finished the half hour like a seasoned politician, fending off every attempt to trap him. A panel of judges would have given him at least a tie. Many listeners felt he did even better than that. He had not hurt his chances of being Bartow County's next commissioner.

Nate took only a few steps outside the radio station when his phone rang. He reached into his pocket to retrieve it. "Hello, Nate Bannister here."

"Nate, you done good. You're goin' to be county commissioner for sure," the voice of a young girl came from the cell phone.

"Is that you, Kid? Did you listen to that slop? That guy was out to get me. You would have been better off outside enjoying this beautiful day the Good Lord gave us rather than listening to such hogwash."

"You showed him, Nate. Nobody is going to manhandle Nate Bannister. Mom said to tell you that you're having supper with us tonight."

"Alright, I'll be home in a couple of hours. I've got some business to take care of before I leave Cartersville. You try to stay out of trouble," he told his little friend.

"You to," she countered. "You'd better if you want to be county commissioner."

Nate was considering a session with Kenneth Cotes, but he thought about the Kid's warning. *I guess I'd better stay out of trouble if I want to be county commissioner.*

CHAPTER 19

Sitting on the brown plaid sofa, in the quietness of his own apartment, Kirby's mind traveled to the place it had difficulty avoiding these days. He reviewed what he knew of the four men he considered suspects in what was now a murder case. The list was compiled based on each man's anti-Nate sentiments. He was assuming the murder was a result of a rift between Houston and his boss.

The mayor seemed like a longshot. Nate was a larger-than-life public figure that people often either liked exceedingly or disliked enormously. Mayor Ellison, like a lot of people, fit into the latter group. He still knew little about Randy Tate, but he found it hard to believe that winning a county election was motive enough to kill and kidnap people. Kenneth Cotes had double motives: greed plus a long-time grudge. These were two possible motives that couldn't be ignored. With Jason Purcell, it was drive for self-elevation, a desire for success and power. He knew that on the surface, it didn't stand out as a glaring reason for murder and destructive behavior, but he also knew that at its extreme, ambition can be a condition that exudes from a form of mental illness. Such a condition can push one to go to whatever ungodly extent necessary to reach his goals. Purcell might be simply a highly motivated normal person. Nothing wrong with that, but . . .

Maybe Houston's death had nothing to do with Nate and the election. The victim wasn't exactly a likeable human being. It is not hard to believe he had enemies, but Kirby's gut told him otherwise. He was sure it was all connected.

Kirby focused on what the boy had seen from his perch in the tree. The shooter wore a green baseball cap. Green and gold happened to be the colors of the Adairsville Tigers, the mascot of the local high school.

It was likely that Mayor Ellison and Kenneth Cotes, both residents of Adairsville, would choose that color for a cap. Tate lived in Cartersville and Purcell was from outside the area. However, Purcell worked for a business that, no doubt, sold caps of various colors, and he might select a green cap to impress the local crowd. Fact was, anyone could have a green cap.

Then there were the sunglasses. No clue there. Most likely all four of the men owned sunglasses. The boy reported that the shooter drove a white car. He didn't know the model or notice anything else about the vehicle. Kirby wished the car had been purple or some color to distinguish it. There are a lot of white cars on the road. With time on his hands, Kirby had done some checking and learned that Randy Tate did not drive a white car, but his wife did. Cotes drove a white pickup. His son, a business partner, owned a white car. Purcell was currently driving a white Toyota rental car, and Mayor Ellison drove a grey SUV. The mayor was the only one of the four that car color seemed to eliminate.

There was one other point the boy made that interested him. The shooter continued to keep the gun pointed in the direction in which he had fired for an extended period. Did that mean anything? Kirby picked up his phone and looked for the number of Victor Dempsey, a profiler with whom he had worked a couple of times in Florida. He was surprised when the state officer answered almost immediately. "Victor, Kirby Gordan here. I know you're a busy man, so I'll get right to the point. Is there anything to learn from a man who freezes in the shooting position for a minute or two after the victim is lying on the ground? Does that suggest anything about the shooter?"

"You're not saying he pointed his weapon down at the fallen body. That would be a normal precaution. You're suggesting he continued to point in the direction in which he had fired the shot?"

"You've got it. Does that tell us anything about the shooter?"

"It might. I would think such a person was savoring the moment. Perhaps he was pleased with himself. He wasn't sure he could do it, but now it was done, and he was patting himself on the back for being the man. This was probably his first time killing. He wasn't a seasoned killer, but now that he's successfully done it, he might do so again. Does that help you any?"

"It gives me more than I had before this phone call."

"I thought you were a businessman, out of police work and living a life of leisure in Georgia."

"That's me. Just helping out where I can. Try to use what you've got, you know."

"I hope you catch him, whoever he is."

"We'll get him. Thanks, Victor."

Kirby's thoughts turned to taking Connie to Atlanta for dinner and a theater production later today. Thinking about that caused him to grin. There was nothing he enjoyed more than being with her. He decided this night would be special. With all the excitement the evening was likely to produce, he hoped he would remember to ask her to once again work her magic with the computer. He wanted her to see if she could find any connection between Houston and any of the suspects. It was a longshot, but he had learned early on that clues were sometimes found in the most unlikely places. He would take care of that on the trip to the city and leave the rest of the evening for greater things. Hopefully a night to remember!

***

Riley was thrilled that Houston's threat was no longer a concern. She could come out of hibernation. That meant running again. Her daily run-and-walk routine was important to both her physical and mental health. She did some of her clearest thinking while doing her road work.

She had pushed the previous mile a little harder than usual. Now she had slowed to a brisk walk. As she often did these days, she thought of Mike. He sure looked good when she and Trish visited with him yesterday. She laughed to herself when she remembered Trish's response to her making that observation after their visit: "He always looks good to me." Trish was right. He did always look good, and she knew that girls noticed.

For the first day or two after Mike's injury, she could only think of what a cruel blow it would be if Mike didn't recover. The two of them would never have a life together. At the time, that thought hurt her deeply. However, as he recovered, she could only focus on how hard it would be to send a husband off each day not knowing if he would return. She wondered, was that the reason she had suppressed their relationship over the past year? Did she unconsciously fear a permanent relationship with someone whose occupation posed such dreadful possibilities? Could that be the reason she blocked Mike's attempt to accelerate their friendship? Did she have an irrational fear of losing what she loved? If so, there was a solution. Mike could step away from law enforcement into a less threatening field, but would he be happy doing something else? Police work had been his dream since childhood. She would never suggest that option to him. She didn't want to be the reason for a man muddling through life, only going through the motions. Yes, it would please her if he chose some safer line of work, but only if that work fulfilled him. Maybe another option would be for her to straighten-up and deal with reality. It was clear that Mike found satisfaction in serving as a policeman. It could be that she needed to accept that and live with it should they decide to tie the knot. For now, she was just glad that he was alive and active again, though still somewhat restricted. Regardless of the turn their relationship would take, she couldn't imagine life without him.

Riley stopped to talk with Amos before entering her own living space. He was busy with one of his favorite chores: giving loving care to his cherished plants and bushes. He had tended to most of them ever since he himself had put them in the ground. "How much did you do today?" he asked her, standing up from the bent position required to pull weeds from around a rose bush.

"I think about four miles, but it was mostly running. Not much walking. I'll get back to my normal five miles in a day or two."

"Good for you. With all that time you spend in a classroom and driving between here and Emory, you need some exercise."

Amos's words were a reminder that, in little more than a month, law school classes would be resuming. She enjoyed her studies and was looking forward to the day she would have that degree, but she wasn't sure she was ready for summer vacation to be over. With all the snags over the last six weeks, she felt that summer vacation had just begun. Trish had been trying to talk her into joining her for the trip to visit their friend in Florida. She had just about decided to take her up on the offer. She needed a vacation, but she cherished the time she had in her little north Georgia nest. She still had a little time to decide. Thanks to Nathan, Trish had not made definite plans for her departure. Riley was genuinely glad. She loved having her special friend with her. As some of the girls used to say in their college days, "Trish was a hoot."

Trish still had not returned from her outing with Nathan when Riley was out of the shower and dressed. Nathan had evening meetings and church activities, so she knew Trish would be available for dinner. She decided she would prepare a nice meal for the two of them. They had mostly eaten sandwiches and such or gone out during Trish's visit. They had also regularly accepted invitations from Amos and Carol. She thought about inviting them to dinner, but decided that this evening, she would like to spend some quality time with her guest. She remembered that one of Trish's favorite meals was lasagna. That's what she would prepare. She would make lasagna, a green salad, and get some Italian bread. They would have to finish it off with apple pie covered with ice cream and a good cup of coffee. Riley had not given a lot of time to developing her kitchen skills, but thanks to her mother's efforts during her late high school days, lasagna was within her capabilities. She needed to go to Food Lion for some of the ingredients she did not have on hand, and she didn't trust herself to make the apple pie. She would find the best store-bought one available. She got into her car and drove the half mile to the supermarket.

While retrieving a grocery cart she ran into Beth Reece. "With Connie away for the evening with your brother, I thought it would be a good time to stock up on groceries," the proud mother reported. "She was really excited about seeing the show at the Fox. She loves that old theater."

"Who wouldn't love such a beautiful old venue? I've only had opportunity to be there twice, but I was duly impressed."

Obviously, Beth didn't want to talk about the theater. Her mind was on the romance. "Do you think we'll be hearing wedding bells anytime soon?" she asked.

Riley played dumb. She knew from her conversations with Kirby that, if he had his way, that event was just around the corner, but it wasn't her place to suggest such possibilities to the mother of the prospective bride. "I don't have any such plans anytime soon," she responded.

"You know what I mean! Have you heard anything about Kirby and Connie settin' the date?" Beth sounded a little irritated with her.

"You'll have to ask your daughter about that. I'm hoping it's going to happen, but I've heard no definite plans."

"Okay. I guess I'd better get on with my grocery shopping." Beth sounded disappointed.

"Good to talk with you, Beth. If you hear anything about a wedding, let me know," she teased. Beth was already pushing her buggy up an isle away from Riley.

It was around six-thirty when Trish appeared in Riley's living room. She stopped, lifted her head, and sniffed. "Is that the marvelous aroma of lasagna I detect?"

"It is, and it should be ready to serve by the time you get washed up."

Trish immediately disappeared and returned in less than three minutes. "How did you know I was hungry? We ate a late lunch, but I just nibbled. Didn't want Nathan to think I'm a heavy eater, even though that tends to be the case sometimes, especially during times of stress."

"Well, this is probably the only time I will prepare your favorite dish while you are here, so I want you to eat hearty."

"No argument here," Trish responded, sitting down at the well-set table. Riley prayed before passing the main dish to her guest.

"Do you mind me asking how the Trish and Nathan relationship is progressing?" Riley asked.

"Like a story straight from one of those Christian romances I used to read. I never dreamed I would find my prince charming down here in the South. Do you think I could be a good preacher's wife?"

"Sounds like it's getting serious," Riley remarked.

"I'm serious, but I don't know how serious he is. I do know he likes me a lot and he kissed me today. I think I might be falling in love."

Riley caught herself before telling her friend to be careful and maybe not to move so fast. *Trish isn't a little girl. She's a young woman mature enough to know how to handle romance. Who am I to offer advice to anyone about relationships?*

They cleaned up the kitchen after the meal and took their apple pie to the living room where they sat and talked well into the night, going back for a second piece of pie before the evening was over. It was like college all over again; one of the most pleasant evenings Riley had experienced in a while. Several times she came close to asking Trish if she thought she had a problem with relationships, but stopped short each time, afraid of the answer she might receive.

***

Kirby had made dinner reservations at the Lawrence, a contemporary restaurant in Midtown. The perfect place for dinner before the play. And he did want the evening to be perfect. He asked for and was given a table away from other diners. After placing their orders, he took Connie's little right hand in his two big ones. "I wanted this to be a truly romantic occasion, but I guess this is about as romantic as I can pull off."

"Oh, this is definitely romantic when you're accustomed to McDonalds in Adairsville," Connie interjected.

"I hope, by now, you are convinced that I love you with all of my heart," Kirby told her.

Beginning to get an idea of where this was going, Connie smiled and looked adoringly into his eyes. "Go on," she said.

He moved his right hand from hers to reach into his pocket. He pulled out a small black case and opened it to reveal a ring that featured a beautiful diamond. "Because you are the love of my life, I want to spend the rest of my life with you. Connie, will you marry me?"

There was a moment of silence. That concerned Kirby at first. He hoped there would be no reluctance. But when he saw the first tears he had ever seen leak from her eyes, he knew the hesitation was not reluctance, but rare emotion from the woman he loved. She swallowed and responded, "Of course I'll marry you. For some time now, I've dreamed and longed for a life as the bride of Kirby Gordan, the finest man I know, and the person I love more than I ever thought it possible to love anyone."

Kirby slipped the ring on her finger and leaned a bit across the table. Their lips met. He had felt those lips against his own numerous times over the past year, but this almost seemed like their first kiss. He had never felt such emotion. They lingered in that position for a moment, oblivious to the people and activity around them. Kirby was sorry for it to end, but he knew there would be a lifetime of such moments in his future.

CHAPTER 20

Kirby called Jason Purcell to ask for a meeting at the property the representative was so desperate to acquire for his company. He led Purcell to believe it was projected building placement in which he was interested, but it was murder in the Oothcaloga cemetery that was really on his mind. Purcell's white Toyota rental was in place when he arrived at the agreed upon spot, but there was no driver in sight. Kirby cautiously exited his own vehicle and looked about with all his senses tuned for possible danger. He heard a bobwhite calling to its mate. Where was Purcell?

Then an abrupt sound like a stick breaking came from directly behind him. He instantly turned to see Purcell standing twenty feet away with a twisted smile on his face and his right hand extended. "Look what I found!" He eagerly showed Kirby his discovery. When Kirby got closer, he could see it was a perfectly crafted arrowhead. "I found it just lying on top of the ground over there beside that little ditch." He pointed to his right.

"Probably was once the sharp end of some Cherokee's arrow. You can still find one now and then. They tell me there was a time when handfuls of them could be found by carefully trawling over certain freshly plowed ground in the area," Kirby said.

"Can I keep it?" Purcell asked. "Since it's on your property, I guess it legally belongs to you."

"Finders keepers," Kirby smiled at him. "It's yours."

Purcell put the found treasure in his pocket. "So, you have some questions about the projected placement of the structures. You understand that at this point nothing is concrete, but the terrain and view from the interstate will naturally dictate much of that. A road will be constructed that will lead from Highway 140 to the top of that hill." He pointed south to the highest peak on the property. "That's where our main store will be located. The parking lot will be huge by Adairsville standards. It will be in both front and back of the attractive building."

Since he had Purcell there under pretense of being interested in the proposed construction, Kirby figured he'd better ask a question or two. "Will there be any buildings other than the main store?"

"Eventually we may put a warehouse building behind the back parking lot. You can be sure it will be tastefully done."

"What about the traffic?" Kirby asked. "Will one road handle the traffic efficiently?"

"There will be two lanes coming in and two going out. We'll, of course, petition the state to put a traffic light at the intersection at Highway 140."

"Sounds like you've got it all figured out," Kirby acknowledged.

"We don't anticipate any problems. This location is perfect for what we have in mind, and I think it will be a tremendous asset to your community. It will be a great way to use this beautiful spot, just sitting here waiting for something good. The only hang up I can see is if Bannister becomes county commissioner. They tell me he is presently running slightly ahead. Maybe if you, as a prominent businessman in the community, would throw your support behind Tate, it would make a difference."

"I'm new to the area, I don't carry any weight in these matters. We'll just have to wait and see. I have confidence the voters know what they're doing. Your being so dead set against Mr. Bannister concerns me. What extent are you willing to go to keep him out of office?"

"I'll do whatever I have to do that's legal to block him."

"What about that which is outside the law? Would you be willing go there?" Kirby asked.

Purcell looked at him suspiciously. "I don't know what you have in mind, I admit to being an aggressive businessman, but I'll not sidestep the law."

"I'm thinking about kidnapping and murder. I'm talking about trying to put the candidate down to get him out of the running."

"Are you out of your mind?" Purcell bellowed. "Do you think I had something to do with kidnapping that child or shooting at that old man? You've got the wrong man. I don't know that I want to do business with you!"

"I'm glad you feel that way, Jason. I was just trying to relieve my own mind. You tell me where you were the afternoon of June twenty-eighth, and we can put this to rest."

"That's no problem. I can tell you exactly where I was. I drove to Augusta for a meeting on the night of the twenty-seventh. I remained there until I retuned on the twenty-ninth. If you need to validate that, I can email you two or three names and numbers of people who were in that meeting."

"If you don't mind, I would appreciate having those. It would eliminate any doubts I have about possibly doing business with you."

"You've got it. I will take care of that as soon as I get back to my room. The names I am supplying are business acquaintances. I would appreciate you not revealing to them that you suspect me of such shady dealings."

"I'll be careful," Kirby told him. "What about Cotes? Have you found him to be honest, or is he the kind of man that might step outside the law to make a dollar or two?"

"I don't know him well, but he seems to me to be an honorable man."

They talked a while longer. Kirby apologized to Purcell for his insinuations. Shortly thereafter, they got into their respective cars and drove away.

Later that day, Kirby received the promised names and phone numbers from Purcell. He called two of the numbers. Without casting any doubt about Purcell's character, he was able to determine that he was in Augusta on the day Houston was shot. That didn't necessarily clear him of spearheading the kidnapping or attempted shooting of Nate, but it seemingly proved he didn't murder the man in the cemetery. *Back to square one. Maybe I'm going totally in the wrong direction. Need to back up and take a new look.*

***

Before going to Calhoun to spend a couple of hours with Mike, Riley and Trish stopped by Bill's place to see how Buster was progressing. When Judy first told them he was not there, they were concerned. Had he left to find a bottle? A moment later, they were elated to learn that he had joined the Cleaning Crew on a job. "Is this the first day he's done that?" Riley asked.

"No. He worked yesterday. Bill said he's a good worker, just ran out of steam before the day was over," Judy told them.

"I can see why that would happen. The way he has lived for the past few years was bound to affect his stamina. It'll take him awhile to get his staying power back," Riley remarked.

"I'm just thankful he's doing something. Idle hands and mind are not good for him. He needs to be busy," Trish reasoned.

"Bill and the guys will keep him active. They know what he needs," Judy commented.

"You're right. They're a lot better equipped than we are to help him. I trust them completely. If anyone can make it happen, they can. You tell Buster we haven't forgotten him. We'll be back soon," Riley told her.

"Tell Buster I'm proud of him and to keep up the good work," Trish added.

"That will thrill him. I think you are the person he most wants to please," Judy told her.

"It's really not me he wants to impress. It's the wife he remembers. I just remind him of her. I suppose in his mind, I sort of represent her. I don't mind that at all if it will help him straighten out his life."

When the two young ladies got to Calhoun, they found Mike sitting on the front porch of his parent's big, colonial style house. "Getting a little air?" Riley asked before leaning over to kiss him.

"I guess I'm getting a little stir crazy. I thought I would come out here for a while before things heat up."

Riley took one of the two empty wicker chairs. "If you two lovers will excuse me, I promised I would call Nathan when we got here," Trish said, taking out her phone and walking to the other side of the porch. "I hope you don't mind Nathan coming by and taking me away for the next hour. He said he had something to show me," she reported when she returned to where her friends were seated.

"I don't mind as long as you allow this lady to stay here with me," Mike said, motioning toward Riley. "I've missed her."

"I don't know how you could miss me. I was here day before yesterday."

"But not yesterday," he groaned. "I get restless if I don't see you every day."

"You're getting spoiled," Riley told him. "You have plenty of people to keep you company."

"But they aren't as beautiful as you. They don't have your magnetic personality, and they don't make me as happy as you do."

"Wow, listen to that. If that isn't a snow job, I've never heard one," Riley laughed.

"Not a snow job, just fact," Mike told her. "You know I can't live without you. Tell her that, Trish. Tell her she'll never find anyone who'll love her more."

Nathan drove into the driveway at that moment. Trish stood and said, "There's my ride. I'm going to stay out of this conversation." She moved toward Nathan's little red car at almost a trot.

"How have you been feeling?" Riley asked.

"Still sore and moving slowly. If I stay seated, it doesn't hurt much, but they tell me I need to spend more time on my feet to eventually eliminate the soreness."

"You do what they tell you, and you'll be back on the job before you know it."

"I don't know, Riley. I've been thinking about that. I don't know if I'm going back to the job. I don't know if police work is for me."

"That's the first time I've heard you talk like that. You've always loved law enforcement. Was it getting wounded while on duty that changed your mind?"

"Sort of. Oh, it's not that I'm now afraid of dying on the job. I'm not a coward. I hope you realize that."

"I know that, Mike. I don't know a braver man."

"I've thought over and over about what happened that night in that yard. What if I had shot and killed the man? I know he was a terrible person, but I still wonder what it would have done to me to know that I had taken a human life. I don't know if I could live with that. I'm not questioning that there are times when, for the protection of innocent people, lives must be taken. I'm questioning whether I'm one who can do it. I don't know." He looked away from Riley.

"What will you do if you leave law enforcement?" Riley asked.

"I don't know, Riley. I'm thinking about working with Dad in the construction business. He's often tried to convince me to do that. He wants to make me a partner. I could take classes at Dalton State and finish that business degree I've worked on from time to time. What do you think, Honey? Would it cause you to think less of me if I quit?"

Think less of him! I would be delighted if he chooses to get out of law enforcement. That's what she wanted to tell him, but she knew she didn't dare. She would not influence him. She wanted him to decide. It had to be his decision. "Of course, I would not be disappointed in you. I want you to do what you are happy doing. If that is police work, then do it. If construction work, then go for it. If you decide on something else, that's okay too."

"Which would you rather marry, a policeman or a construction worker?" Mike asked with a sheepish smile on his face.

"When I marry, what a man does for a living will not be a factor. I will marry because I love that man and have decided I cannot live without him," She quickly replied.

"I'm glad to know that, because at this point, I'm having a hard time settling on a definite plan for my future. Getting to know Nathan has sparked another possibility, though I'm not crazy about the timeline required. I've entertained the idea of finishing my bachelors and then going on to seminary with the idea of becoming a pastor. I know your dad was a pastor. Do you think that would be realistic for me? Is it something I can handle?"

"Mike, I know you could be successful in any career you chose. You would be a magnificent pastor if the Lord is leading you in that direction."

"So how do I determine if he is calling me? Is there some kind of formula for deciding that?" he asked.

"Not that I'm aware of. Dad used to say when you try to find the Lord's will, and the answer isn't in the Bible, make it a matter of prayer, and the Lord will in some way lead you. It's always worked for me. That's how I ended up in law school."

"How did the Lord convince you that he wanted you to be an attorney?" Mike asked almost before she got the statement out of her mouth.

"Looking good, Mike," a male voice called from the driver's side of a slow-moving vehicle passing by. Mike waved.

"That's Pervis Johnson, a classmate of mine in high school. He lives a few doors down. Pervis never had a problem figuring out what he wanted to do. He's an assistant manager at Chic-Fil-A. He'll have his own store in a couple of years."

"To answer your question, Mike, I prayed for several months about what the Lord's will was for my life. I thought he might be calling me to be a missionary, but at some point, law became the only option. He closed some doors and opened others. I began to have a peace about going to law school that I did not feel about any other direction I could've taken. I still don't know why that's where the Lord chose to put me, but I'm confident it's his will for me."

"Well, it gives me a lot to think about. I guess I have some time to decide. They aren't expecting me back at the station for several weeks. I'll be sitting around drawing my disability for a while. Plenty of time to think and pray."

"I don't know a better way to use your time," Riley told him. "Speaking of knowing the Lord's will, what do you think about Nathan and Trish? Is there something serious going on there? Do you really think they might become an item?"

"I don't think they are *becoming* an item. I think they *are* an item. Nathan is smitten. He tells me he loves the girl," Mike told her. "I guess it would be a little quick to expect to see a ring on her finger before she leaves, but I'm betting it won't be long. How is Trish interpreting their relationship? Is it just fun and games for her, or is she taking it seriously?"

"From what I've been able to get out of her, she feels just like Nathan."

"How do you feel about that?" Mike asked.

"They are two fine people. I'm glad they have found one another, but I hope they don't do anything hastily."

"Sometimes hasty is a good thing," Mike remarked.

Riley looked at him but did not reply.

Trish and Nathan were well over an hour returning, but that was okay with Riley. She enjoyed her time with Mike on the front porch. Mike's mother came out of the house in the last ten minutes to say hello.

Driving back to Adairsville, Riley asked, "Well, Trish, are you going to tell me what Nathan had to show you?"

"Sure, I'll tell you. He showed me the apartment he will be moving into in a couple of weeks. It's much bigger than the one he is presently living in."

"Does the fact it is bigger mean anything?" Riley asked.

"It means he is going to have more room," Trish answered, and then changed the subject.

CHAPTER 21

Amos and Carol were leaving city hall, where they had taken care of some personal business. "Let's walk down to Bradley Farms," Amos suggested to his wife.

"I know why you want to go to that bakery. I think, maybe, we need to stay away from there. You don't need ice cream." Besides offering great baked goods, Bradley Farms also had the best ice cream in town, and Amos loved ice cream. Sometimes he hated the fact that his wife knew him so well.

"Who said I want ice cream?"

"After all these years with you, you don't have to tell me what's on your mind."

"What's on my mind now, old girl?" He kissed his wife on the cheek while they were still walking.

"Stop that! Someone will see," she scolded.

"So what, we're married. Let them look. Maybe it'll inspire them."

"I think you're entering your second childhood," Carol barked as they entered the front door to Bradley Farms Baked Goods. When they came out to the sidewalk to sit on the bench in front of the store, they both had an ice cream cone.

"I thought you said ice cream wasn't good for you," Amos remarked.

"I said it wasn't good for *you*," she replied. "I didn't say it was bad for me."

"What's the difference? Why is it bad for me and not you?"

"Look down, old man. Look at that waistline and you'll see why you don't need those extra calories."

"Okay," Amos drew the word out, glaring at his wife who was more than a little past her ideal weight. "Well, look who's coming. I bet the Kid has a hankerin' for ice cream too."

Carol looked up to see Nate and the Kid headed their way. "Hello Amos, Carol," Nate said, nodding before following the Kid through the door. Kaylene seemed to be in a hurry.

"Good day for an ice cream cone, isn't it?" Amos remarked.

"Any day is a good day for ice cream according to the Kid," Nate replied.

"That's sort of the way Amos sees it too," Carol said.

"Good to see things back to normal, isn't it? I missed seeing those two strolling the streets during all the trouble," Amos declared. "Now that you've had a night to sleep on it, how do you feel about what we discussed last night?"

"You mean about moving out of the church and into a house? I'd rather just stay where we are until we can no longer climb the stairs. I think Kirby and Riley still need us around for a while. I know I've really become attached to them. It's like living under the same roof with family."

"Good. Then we agree. I do feel that we should give them the option since I'm retiring. I guess its possible they want to give our place to someone else."

"It's possible, but I've not heard any hints like that from them. From everything I've heard them say, they're happy with the present arrangement," Carol assured him.

"If it's right for them, then it's right for me," Amos concluded.

Nate and the Kid came out of the store; both had an ice cream cone in their right hands. "The Kid twisted my arm," Nate muttered as he went by, holding up the cone slightly.

"I bet she didn't have to twist it much," Amos responded.

"Do you think they will ever catch the person who was behind the kidnapping?" Carol asked after the old man and young girl were out of hearing distance.

"Sure, they will!" Amos replied. "They'll get him, and I would be surprised if it's not soon. Kirby is on it like a bloodhound after a rabbit. When he's on something, he doesn't let up until he gets his man. They tell me that while a detective down in Florida, he solved just about every case he was on. They came to a place where they were giving him all the hard ones because they knew he could get the job done."

"Who told you that, old man? You haven't talked with anyone he worked with down there. How could you know that?"

"Trust me. I just know."

They chatted for a few more minutes on the bench before taking their conversation to the car to head for Rome. They had some shopping to do.

***

Since shooting Houston, the man with the slicked back hair had experienced contradicting emotions. Sometimes he was rather proud of his ability to carry out his mission. It had to be done and he did it. At other times he had pangs of conscience. Had he actually shot another human being? He toyed with the idea of taking care of Bannister himself, but, thus far, it had not gotten past the planning stage. He knew a little about the old man's habits. It wouldn't be hard to catch him in a vulnerable spot. He kept remembering Houston's insistence that the former ballplayer was somehow indestructible. He knew Bannister well enough to know he wasn't guarded by any divine presence. It didn't make any difference that he had been a star baseball player. He would bleed like everyone else.

He sometimes worried that Houston would somehow be traced back to him. He had decided he didn't have a lot to worry about from the local authorities. The county sheriff wasn't the sharpest knife in the drawer, and the Adairsville police chief was just a kid. It was Gordan snooping around that worried him most. He didn't know a great deal about him, but he knew he had been a detective somewhere down in Florida. He also remembered that Gordan had nailed his own uncle's murderer. The man would have to do his best to stay clear of him. *If Houston had not stirred him up, I'd probably be home free.*

Maybe he didn't have to worry about Bannister. Polls showed the race was still too close to call. Perhaps the voters would come though. But would that be enough? Not after what he did! Simply losing the election wouldn't be enough. He had to be punished more severely than that. He felt his rage starting to boil again. It seemed to happen almost every time he thought about the candidate. It took all his willpower to keep his feelings under wraps. He knew he had to appear to be an upright citizen if he was to reach his goals. He would go about his normal routine and forget about the whole mess, at least for now. He could decide his next move tomorrow.

***

It was the third time in two days that Kirby had unsuccessfully tried to set up an appointment with Kenneth Cotes. Cotes's secretary kept giving him the runaround. The latest excuse was that some family deal had come up. Maybe Cotes wasn't the man, but he was sure making it hard for Kirby to eliminate him. *I'm about to run out of suspects. It's not my worry anyway. I need to let Charley and his boys take care of it. They haven't asked for my help. I'm just butting in where I'm not wanted.*

Kirby had talked Connie into taking the afternoon off. There were some things he wanted to discuss with her. He thought a ride into the north Georgia hills would be the perfect way to approach it. Except for those places where they had business interests, he was still relatively unfamiliar with the state. Connie recommended Cloudland Canyon, a beautiful state park near Lafayette. They could be there in a couple of hours, and she insisted the drive would be beautiful. Kirby discovered that she wasn't wrong, but then he had known for some time that she was seldom wrong with any of her appraisals. She had to know she was right before speaking up. If she wasn't sure, she simply kept her opinion to herself. She had a sharp mind and was sure of herself. Of course, she was a beauty, but Kirby had learned there were a lot of beautiful women in the world. The trick was finding one who was beautiful as well as possessing other desirable assets. Kirby knew he had found such a lady in Connie. She would probably be intimidating to some guys, but Kirby decided she was perfect for him. They had taken a year to decide if they were compatible and now there was no doubt.

The year not only gave them opportunity to know each other better, but it had been a time of spiritual development for both. Kirby had found his way back to the Lord. Connie had accepted the Lord just five months previously, being baptized on a Sunday morning. Both were demonstrating significant spiritual growth. They understood that would be vital to a successful marriage.

"There're a couple of decisions we need to make," Kirby said as he drove down the narrow highway. "We need to decide what you're going to do about work once we're married. It doesn't matter to me. I would be happy to have you continue to oversee our business affairs. You have done a great job. Should you decide to give that up, it will be difficult to replace you. On the other hand, if you decide you don't want to work after marriage, that's fine with me. I just want you to be a happy wife."

"I've thought a lot about it over the last two or three days. I think I would like to step down from my present position. However, I don't want to totally step away from it all. I figure bein' your partner in life will spill over into our business interests. As you obviously know, I have a real interest in such matters, and I think I have somethin' to offer. I'm marryin' a fairly well-to-do gentleman, so I don't think I'm goin' to need a paycheck."

"Whatever you are comfortable with will work for me. Another decision is about where we'll live after we're married. We need to decide that now because there could be major preparation required. We can go in one of several directions. You can move in with me at our . . ." Kirby paused. "What shall I call it? Church compound. We could look around and try to locate an existing house that will make you happy, or, as you know, we have a lot of property. I'm sure we can find a place on which to build a new house just the way you want it. As you said earlier, you're marrying a fairly well-to-do man. A couple of years ago, I couldn't have made such a promise, but, thanks to Uncle James, I can tell you that I would love to build you your dream house."

"Wow. That sounds so wonderful. Eventually, let's do that. Let's build our dream house together. But first, I think I would like to move into your apartment in the church. It's so quaint and cozy. I would love bein' under the same roof with people I love so much. I know that in time we'll need more room. Certainly, when we have a child."

"And I hope that won't be long," Kirby remarked.

"I'm in agreement with you about that. Maybe after a year or so to enable us to adjust as a couple, we could start thinkin' about children," Connie said.

"And, of course, the time will probably come when we'll need to provide living accommodations for your mother. You know I have become extremely fond of her."

"Oh, yes, my mother. She'll live in the family house alone, as long as she dares. Right now, she's fine, but I don't know how long it will be before she's goin' to need to have someone around to watch her. We'll have to drag her away from that house kickin' and screamin' when the time comes." They continued to talk about such matters and enjoyed the scenery until they arrived at the park.

"It's nice," Kirby remarked, looking around.

"You haven't seen anything yet. Wait until we go down into the canyon. It's gorgeous, one of the more beautiful sights in the whole state."

"You mean we're going to walk down there?" Kirby pointed in the direction of the canyon.

"Of course, we are. You can't come to Cloudland Canyon without goin' down to the waterfall. The trail's right over there." She pointed to her left.

"You remember that I have a wounded right leg, don't you?"

"That happened a year ago. Your leg is fine. Getting the exercise will be good for it. Don't give me a lot of excuses. You're goin' to see the waterfall at the bottom of the canyon. Besides, it's a romantic spot," she added with a wink.

"Can't turn down an invitation like that. I'm glad I wore my walking shoes," he added.

The trip down the narrow trail was not nearly as treacherous as Kirby had thought it would be. What they found at the bottom was like a beautiful painting. Water falling from far above, forming a pool perhaps the size of the typical public swimming pool. There was a sign prohibiting swimming, but several boys, who looked to be middle school age, were ignoring the sign, having a great time in the water. "It's everything you said it was," Kirby remarked, eyes fixed on the picture postcard scene before him. "In the years ahead, we'll see a lot of beautiful places together. You can show me the out-of-the-way places in Georgia, and I'll take you to New England. Together, we can visit anywhere you want to go in the world."

"It all sounds so wonderful. Even without such promises, I would still be the happiest girl in the world. I never dreamed I'd spend the rest of my life with someone so thoughtful, loving, and handsome," she added before turning and embracing him. What followed was another of those wonderful kisses that seemed to turn Kirby's world upside down. When they released one another and took a few steps toward a large rock to use it as a seat, they noticed three of the boys standing in the water gawking at them while giggling. They sat on the rock for over an hour, holding hands and talking of the future, before walking back up the trail and to Kirby's car. It had been a pleasant day for both future bride and groom.

CHAPTER 22

The morning sun was already bright on this July Georgia day as Kirby and Amos rode past the pastures just west of Adairsville. Kirby wanted to drive his car, but Amos insisted that where they were going was pickup country. "The boys did a great job of tearin' down the old shack," Amos told him. "If it weren't for a pile of bricks from the chimney, you'd never know there was a house there. I didn't want to dispose of them since people like to use antique brick. I'll find someone who'll haul them away. It's a beautiful piece of property. You know, it's where all that mess with the Kid started for Riley. It was there that I spotted Kaylene in the back seat of that car."

"I remember," Kirby said. "The girls are still talking about the adventure of coming out here that night to search. Sometimes I think we need to put an anchor on Riley. Can't stay out of trouble."

"To her credit, it always seems to be someone else's trouble she's trying to fix," Amos said.

"I know. She has a heart for people, and I appreciate that, but that doesn't cancel out the danger. She's drawn to it like a baby to milk. I shudder to think what it's going to be like when she starts her law practice. I see her being totally hands-on in every case she accepts. That's why I'm trying to direct her into business law, but she'll have none of that. She wants to help people who're in trouble."

"Well, you can't fault her for that. The world would be a better place if everyone had a heart like hers," Amos declared.

"You're right, but that doesn't make it any easier to protect her, especially since she rejects the whole idea of needing protection. It's hard to safeguard someone who insists they can take care of themselves."

"But you've got to admit she's done a pretty good job of that," Amos insisted. "I think I just need to be her friend and you, her brother. I've been thinkin' about it and have come to the conclusion that she's a strong young lady who's goin' to handle life with the proper wisdom, grace, and strength. We can be there for her when things break down, and I know she'll be there for us when we need her assistance."

Is he scolding me for being an overprotective brother? Kirby was silent for the next couple of minutes. Then they took the dirt and gravel drive that ran off the paved road. When they came over the little hill, Kirby was in awe. It was one of the most charming sights he had ever seen. "Look at that little hill over there with the big oak tree. Wouldn't that be the perfect place for a house? I can visualize a two-story brick colonial sitting behind that big tree."

"That's where the old house stood," Amos told him. "See the bricks stacked over to the right?"

"I can see it now!" Kirby was obviously excited about what he saw. "I see stables down behind the house, and maybe an arena. There would be a few horses. No reason for stables and arena if you don't have horses. But I'm getting ahead of myself. I promised Connie that when we build a house, it would be her dream house. I'll have to get her out here to see what she thinks."

"You wouldn't have any problems with the neighbors out here. There are none to speak of," Amos said. "You're right. That little hill would look great decorated with a beautiful new house."

Amos parked the truck. They got out to walk around the property. Kirby and Riley had owned this site for almost a year, yet he had never set foot on it. There were several hundred additional undeveloped acres that belonged to them that he had never explored. There might be other locations more suitable for a home than this one, but he doubted it.

"So, are you and Connie planning to build a new home?" Amos asked.

"We'll probably eventually do that, but, for a time, I think we'll live in my place. Connie likes the idea of having you guys as same-building neighbors. Waiting to settle into a more permanent place will allow us to give more consideration to what we want. Maybe keep us from making some mistakes."

"Sounds like a sound plan to me." Amos nodded his head. "So, it will be alright for me and Carol to stay where we are, for a time."

"Alright? We would be upset if you decided to go elsewhere. We want you to remain there for as long as you wish."

"We love being there, and I would hate to leave my garden and all the things that grow on the property. The only thing that concerns me about the arrangement is that Carol and I are slowing down considerably. We don't like to admit it, but we don't know how much longer we can climb those stairs. Both of us are still handling them fairly well, but it may be a different story this time next year."

"I've thought about that. As I see it, if you folks agree to stay, we can handle that problem in one of two ways. I can give you my apartment downstairs when Connie and I build our house. It's about the same size as yours, and with the study, a little larger. The other option is that we install an elevator or chairlift."

"An elevator would be an expensive solution. I would hate to see you spend that kind of money on our behalf."

"It would be to our advantage to keep you there. You've made us a lot more money than what an elevator would cost. It's your home and we want you to stay there as long as you wish."

"Thank you for that, Kirby. We just didn't want to impose."

"Far from imposing, you have been and continue to be a huge asset. We love both of you and consider you family. Incidentally, unless she changes her mind, Connie will step down from her position with the estate after we are married. I would appreciate you starting to think about someone to take her place. We're going to need someone with a bookkeeping background, but you know that. You know better than anyone else what we need."

"I'll give it some thought. We may have to go to an agency to find someone."

Amos drove them back home, where Kirby got into his own car to make a trip to the barbershop. He needed a haircut, but he had also learned that a visit there once every two or three weeks allowed him to stay current with local news.

The talk at the shop today covered most of the rumors about the murder in the Oothcaloga cemetery. The most recent version was a yarn about the killing being the result of an attempt to bring big time organized crime to Adairsville. "How do you feel about that, Gordan? You're the crime expert," Ray Watson, a local auto parts store manager, asked.

"You know about as much as I know about it. I'm just a lumber and hardware man," Kirby responded. *Where do people get these ideas?*

Another theory receiving consideration at the barbershop was that Houston was shot by the husband of his current girlfriend. *I guess some people need a little sensationalism in their lives.*

Before leaving town, Kirby would stop by Connie's office. He wanted to tell her about the impression the property he and Amos had visited made on him, but first he would drop in on Davis Morgan at his bookshop to see if he might have a good book that would give him an overview of Georgia history. "How's business?" he asked when he saw Davis leaning over a shelf of books.

"Today's sales aren't going to make me rich. In fact, they might not be sufficient to pay for my gas home tonight, and as you know, I live just across the railroad tracks."

"Well, maybe I can help out a little. I'm looking for a book on Georgia history. I thought I needed to learn something about the state in which I'm now living."

"That's a good ambition," the bookseller said. "Let's go over here to the Georgia section," he suggested, leaving his crutches in a nearby chair to wobble the few feet to his destination.

"I'm impressed. That's a pretty strong effort from a man who isn't supposed to walk again," Kirby remarked.

"I'm making some progress but still have a way to go. This thing has taught me patience like no other challenge I've had."

"It hasn't whipped you though. You're an inspiration to a lot of us. Keep up the good work. You're getting there."

Davis showed him the Georgia section. Kirby browsed for a few minutes before leaving with a copy of Kenneth Coleman's *A History of Georgia*, as well as the semi-rare *History of Bartow County* by Lucy Josephine Cunyus. He also had eighty dollars less in his billfold.

From there, Kirby went down the street and up the stairway to Connie's office. "I was about to call you," she announced with some urgency as he entered the room. "You remember asking me to see if I could find any connection between Houston and any of your suspects? Well, I've been workin' on that today."

"What, not even a hello or 'I like your new haircut' for your fiancé?"

"We can take care of the salutations later. Come over here and look at this." She pointed at the screen of her computer, which showed a genealogy tree. "Guess who're cousins?" She looked up at him and smiled.

Kirby's eyes closely examined the page. "We've found our man," he declared. "It has to be him. And he was barely on my list."

CHAPTER 23

With the latest development, Kirby was convinced that Randy Tate was his man, but he had no real evidence to turn over to the authorities as of yet. Perhaps he could get him to slip up and incriminate himself. He wanted to wrap up this whole mess now. He got out of his car in front of Tate's office. "You two wait here," he instructed Amos and Bill, who had also started to climb out of the vehicle. "If I'm not back in a half hour, call the sheriff and tell him what we know and that I need some help."

"Don't you think at least one of us ought to go with you?" Amos suggested.

"I've got a better chance of getting him to talk if I'm alone. This is what I used to do, you know." While walking toward the office building, Kirby felt a little doubt about his ill-conceived plan. He was no longer a cop. Maybe he should let the proper authorities take care of this. But then he was at the door. No turning back now.

It was still business hours. Kirby walked through the unlocked front door. There was no receptionist behind the desk in the front office. He remembered from his last visit which door led to Tate's office. He knocked on that door. After a moment it opened. A surprised Tate stood in front of him with the hint of a smile on his face.

"Sorry to bother you, sir," Kirby said, "but there was no one out front. May I take a few moments of your time?"

"Why, of course," the insurance agent answered, and stepped out of the doorway. He motioned for Kirby to come in. "Have a seat." He pointed toward a chair in front of the desk. "Pam, my receptionist, has a sick child, so I let her go home a little early today. What can I help you with?"

"I just need to ask you a few questions."

"Sure, still trying to sort out the commissioner question?" Tate asked.

"No, not exactly. It's true I'm trying to do some sorting, but not so much about the coming election. I was wondering where you were late afternoon on June the twenty-eighth?"

"Why do you need to know that?" Tate asked. All his previous charm suddenly disappeared.

"It's important because that's the day a man named Houston was killed in a cemetery in Adairsville. A man who happened to be your cousin. Killed by a man wearing sunglasses and a green baseball cap, like those over there," Kirby added, pointing toward a green cap and a pair of sunglasses lying side by side atop a piece of office furniture.

"Are you accusing me of murder?" Tate almost shouted the question.

"I'm just asking some questions, trying to get to the bottom of a very messy affair. Do you mind answering my question?"

"What right do you have to interrogate me? You have no authority here. I'm of a mind to report you for harassment."

"You go right ahead and call the sheriff. We can talk with him together. When he hears what I have to tell him, he'll certainly want to talk with you. Now, are you going to answer my question? Where were you on the afternoon of the twenty-eighth of June?"

"I'm sure I have that information here in my day planner, but I don't see that it's any of your business."

"It's my business because my sister was placed in great danger. A friend of ours, a young girl, was kidnapped, and an attempt was made on the life of another friend who happens to be your opponent in an upcoming election. Yes, I'd say it's my business."

Tate was now breathing hard with a look of panic on his face. "Okay, I can prove I had nothing to do with Houston's death or any of the other things you are accusing me of. Let me get my day planner." He reached to open a desk drawer.

By the tone of his voice, Kirby immediately suspected Tate was up to no good, but it was too late to do anything to stop him. Instead of a day planner, the insurance agent pulled a gun from the drawer and pointed it toward Kirby. "If you had minded your own business and kept your nose out of my affairs, we could have avoided all this," he nervously declared. His right hand, which held the gun, shook noticeably. "I didn't plan to kill anyone. I just offered to pay Houston to put Bannister out of the election. He couldn't get anything right. He made a mess of the whole matter, and then he threatened to expose me if I didn't keep giving him money. I didn't doubt that he would keep squeezing me for the rest of his life, so I had to end it right then and there."

"Is being county commissioner that important to you?" Kirby asked.

"I want to be commissioner, but that's not what this is about. I could live with just running my business and someday retiring with sufficient resources to live well for the rest of my life. I don't necessarily need to win that election."

"Then what is it about?" Kirby calmly asked.

"You thought you had it all figured out, didn't you? Well, apparently there's a part of the story you don't know. The most important part."

"I wish you would tell me about it."

"I guess you have the right. No reason to keep it a secret from you now. It started about thirteen years ago. Do you remember me telling you I had a son who died?

"Yes, I remember," Kirby quietly responded.

"He was our youngest child and the apple of his mother's eye. I loved him too. He was special, such a gentle boy. Eddie loved baseball. His dream was to someday play major league baseball. He once had the opportunity to meet Nate Bannister at an awards banquet. I guess it was because Bannister was local and had once been a star of sorts that caused Eddie to idolize him. He read everything he could get his hands on about the old fool. He had his room decorated with pictures and posters of him. We couldn't sit down at the table for dinner without the boy telling us some story about Nate. To be honest, we got tired of hearing about Nate Bannister, but we tolerated it because he was the boy's hero."

A sound came from the other side of the office door. Tate got up from his chair and walked around the desk, keeping his eyes on Kirby and the gun pointed in his direction. "You stay where you are," he demanded before cracking the door to look around. He flashed a nervous smile and closed the door. "Just the office cat," he explained, walking back to his place behind his desk. Again, he was seated in the chair.

"You were telling me about Eddie," Kirby calmly reminded him.

"Well, Eddie got sick, and we learned he had leukemia. They told us there was no possibility of doing anything that could save him. He wasn't a candidate for any treatment. He started going downhill quickly. We just wanted to keep him with us as long as possible. Then he got really bad and was in the hospital in Atlanta. We stayed there with him night and day, trying to make him as comfortable as possible. Someone on staff at the hospital learned that Eddie had this thing about Bannister. He made some contacts to get him to come and spend some time with Eddie. We were told he would be there late one Thursday afternoon. I don't think I had ever seen Eddie as excited as he was that day. He was going to get to spend time with his hero. But four o'clock came, the time Bannister was supposed to come, then five and ultimately six, and still no Bannister. When we inquired, we were told he had an emergency and would reschedule. I'd never seen a boy so disappointed. A little after eleven that very evening, he was gone. I have no doubt that had Bannister kept his word instead of going out carousing somewhere, we would have had our boy for at least a few more days."

There was a moment of silence and Tate looked down at the desk briefly before catching himself. He quickly jerked his head up again to keep an eye on his prisoner. "When I heard he had his heart set on county commissioner, I immediately knew I had to run against him. To beat him would be one way of getting even with him for what he did to Eddie. Then it began to look as if he might win. There was no way I was going to let that happen. I made a business trip to Macon where I inadvertently ran into Houston. Even though he was a cousin, I didn't know him well, but I had heard a lot of talk from family members about the kind of man he was. When we talked, he made it clear he needed money. It occurred to me that this could be my answer. When I explained to him what I had in mind, he immediately told me he would do it for a price. And the price wasn't bad. I didn't know at the time that he would keep messing things up while all the while increasing the price."

"So you killed him," Kirby accused. "You made arrangements to meet him in the cemetery, drove your wife's car to Adairsville, and shot him dead."

"I didn't mean for anyone to die. He had to be stopped," Tate said.

"You need to think about what you are about to do," Kirby suggested. "Any jury would be sympathetic when they understand what Houston did to you. After all, it's pretty clear he beat his wife to death and shot a police officer."

"Did he?" the man with the gun asked. "I didn't know his wife."

"It sure seems that way. You turn yourself over to the sheriff and surely they will take all that into account." Of course, Kirby made no mention of Tate's part in the kidnapping and attempt on Nate's life. He knew that alone would put Tate away for several years. He was banking on him, in his current state of mind, to overlook that. "Why don't you give me the gun. We can go down to the sheriff's office together. The fact is you can't get out of this building without being apprehended anyway. Two capable gentlemen are waiting for me outside. If I'm not out there in another five minutes or so, they will call the sheriff and then come in searching for me. You don't want a scene like that, do you? You don't want to kill anyone else and put your family through such an ordeal. Why don't you give me the gun and turn yourself in? Let's end it right here."

There was a period of silence in which Tate's face exhibited a faraway look. Kirby wasn't sure if he would surrender or start shooting. He braced himself as a minute or two passed.

Finally, Tate took a step toward him and handed him the gun. "I guess you're right. No reason to take this any further. I can't win." Kirby breathed easier, and then he saw tears coming from the eyes of the man who had so brazenly shot his cousin in the back three times a few days earlier. It was over.

CHAPTER 24

It was a beautiful summer morning in Adairsville, just a little past nine o'clock. Trish had announced the previous day that she would be leaving to continue her trip to Florida around ten. Riley had hoped Trish would stop to spend another day or two with her on her way back home, but as much as she wanted to do that, Trish was sticking to her commitment to take the eastern route home so she could stop to visit a beloved aunt.

Then it started. The first of a long procession of people rang Riley's doorbell. Naturally, Nathan was first, there to bid his newfound love farewell, at least for now. Earlier they had made plans for him to journey north in the late fall to meet her parents. He embraced her when he entered the room. If Riley had any doubts about the deep feelings the two had for one another, those uncertainties disappeared when she saw the way their eyes met.

Next to arrive were Kirby and Connie. Connie, sporting her new diamond on her ring finger, remarked, "I couldn't let my little sleuth partner get away without giving her a big hug."

Amos and Carol showed up, Carol carrying a plate of brownies and assorted goodies. "I thought you might enjoy some snacks for the road," she told Trish before giving her one of her special prolonged hugs. "We've loved having you here. We hope you'll return soon. You know how to liven things up, and I like that."

Mike also came, still moving slower than normal, but with a handsome smile plastered across his face.

"You shouldn't be here. You ought to be saving your strength for more important things," Trish told him. They hugged, and Trish whispered into his ear so only he could hear, "Don't give up on Riley. I know she loves you."

"Thank you, Trish. I don't intend to. I appreciate your encouragement," Mike replied.

It was the last visitors to arrive that surprised everyone. Riley opened the door to let Jessie and Buster into the room. Buster was clean shaven and wearing clothes obviously borrowed from either Bill or Jessie. They were a little too large for him. "We are on our way to a job," Jessie announced, "but when Buster heard Trish was leaving today, he insisted on coming to say goodbye."

Buster looked at Trish and, suddenly, the first real smile any of them had witnessed from him came across his face. When Trish, the girl who normally showed little emotion, saw the smile, she lost it. Tears streamed down her cheeks. She covered the five steps toward Buster with rapid strides and wrapped both arms around him, holding tightly the man she had previously hesitated to touch.

"I owe you so much," Buster told her in a strong voice she had not heard from him before. "You're the one who got me off the bottle. I don't think I could've done it without you. It's hard, and I'm takin' it day by day, but so far, so good."

"You'll do it. I know you will. You've got the Good Lord on your side, and he can do anything." She glanced at Riley, then back at Buster. "I want you to know you have taught me a lot. I will never forget you," she assured him before kissing him on the cheek.

It was slightly past ten o'clock when Trish finally said with some reluctance, "I've delayed long enough. I'm going to have to get on the road."

"Could we send you off right?" Amos asked. "Maybe, we could join hands and give thanks for the friendship the Lord has blessed us with." They formed a circle and Amos began to pray. "Lord, we thank you for sending this lovely little lady our way. We thank you for what she has contributed to each of our lives. There's so much we would have missed had we never had the opportunity to know her. Thank you for all the good she has accomplished in this place. You have blessed us by her very presence. May she continue to grow strong in you and be the kind of person she has proven to be during these weeks with us, one who cares fervently about people.

"Father, we feel strongly that you have something special in store for Trish. Help her to find your direction for her life and give her the strength to live it. She's important to us. We ask that you give her a safe journey, and someday soon bring her safely back to us. We pray these things in the name of Christ. Amen!"

There was a chorus of amens when Amos completed his prayer. Then another round of hugs, and Trish was on her way, a better person for her time with some pretty remarkable people.

***

It was two days after Trish left town. Kirby was at a table at the Little Rock with a cup of coffee. An early afternoon break at Adairsville's favorite little café was fast becoming a ritual for the young detective-turned-businessman. He usually ended up in an enjoyable conversation with someone he had not known before. Today would be no exception. Nate Bannister came into the dining room of the popular establishment in the calm that followed the chaos of the lunch hour. Kirby had seen Nate a few times around town and at church. Baseball being his game, he had known about Bannister's career long before he and Riley came to the little north Georgia town that had become their home.

Bannister looked his way, then walked toward him. "You're Kirby Gordan, aren't you?" he asked before extending his hand. "I'm Nate Bannister, Adairsville, Georgia. I want to thank you. I understand you're the man who exposed Tate for the charlatan he turned out to be."

"I guess I had a part in it. There were several people who contributed to solving the case. Sit down, Mr. Bannister. Join me for a cup of coffee."

"That's why I'm here," the older gentleman declared, pulling up a chair. As soon as he was seated, a waitress was at his side. He ordered coffee and remarked to Kirby, "I guess I'll be county commissioner by default now that the other man is out of the race."

"You don't sound so happy about that," Kirby responded.

"I don't know if I am. It all seems a little overwhelming for an old baseball player like me."

"I've heard that no job is too big for Nate Bannister," Kirby responded with a grin.

"You've been talking with the Kid. That's what she thinks, and, I suppose, I've never bothered to discourage that idea. I kind of like havin' her think that. She's like a daughter to me, you know."

"Yes, I'm aware of that. I guess you've heard that Tate's anger toward you stimmed from years ago when you didn't show up to spend some time with his dying son. Do you remember that incident?"

The old man was silent for a moment before his eyes again focused on Kirby across the table. "You know, at first I didn't, but after thinking about it for a time I made the connection. Yes, he was right. I didn't get there when I said I would. I did go to the hospital the next day but was told by a nurse that the boy had died in the night. I was too late." The elderly gentleman went silent, looking down at the table until the waitress brought his coffee. "Thank you, young lady," he said softly.

"Nate, I'm not trying to be unkind or judgmental, but my curiosity compels me to ask why you didn't make it to the hospital to visit the boy that night."

More silence. Then the old man spoke, "It was the night the Kid was born. I felt duty-bound to go to the hospital in Rome. I sat in the waiting room until after she came into the world. For me, it was a night to remember." Nate paused for a moment before continuing in his quiet, raspy voice, "And I guess I can see how Tate couldn't forget it either."

AFTERWORD

With the arrest of Randy Tate, the Gordan siblings have brought another Adairsville caper to a successful conclusion. However, there is unfinished business, and who knows what mystery will pop up next in little Adairsville, Georgia. It looks like Kirby and Connie are on the way to the altar, but nothing has been settled with Riley and Mike. Can Riley shake her demons? Will Mike remain on the Adairsville police force, or will he decide to go in another direction? Will there be a new business partner coming on board when Connie is married? Will Buster remain on the wagon now that Trish has left town? Did you ever wonder about the past of the Cleaning Crew? All questions that demand yet another volume in the Adairsville Heritage Mystery Series. . . .

Speaking of Adairsville! You ought to see what's happening in our little town. Buildings are being restored in the old business district, with new buildings and houses popping up all over town. Our depot hosts a wonderful little museum. And can you believe it? The Little Rock Café has reopened. I know in our books, it never closed. It's been an integral part of our stories, but it actually closed years ago. It's back in a big way. When you visit us, you'll want to stop by and visit Little Rock proprietor Jim Pinkard to sample some of the great food he offers.

Yes, a lot of exciting things are happening. The fall would be a great time to take that detour off Highway 75 to come see what we are about. Or maybe spring, winter, or even summer when Riley is home from law school.

If it sounds like we're mixing fiction and reality, it's true. We've been doing that for a while now.

Printed in the United States
by Baker & Taylor Publisher Services